C. S. LEWIS

Screwtape Proposes a Toast

and other pieces

Collins

FOUNT PAPERBACKS

First published in Fontana Books 1965
Reprinted in Fount Paperbacks January 1977
Nineteenth impression November 1987

Printed and bound in Great Britain by
William Collins Sons & Co. Ltd, Glasgow

SCREWTAPE
PROPOSES A TOAST

and other pieces

Born in Ireland in 1898, C. S. Lewis was educated at Malvern College for a year and then privately. He gained a triple First at Oxford and was a Fellow and Tutor at Magdalen College 1925–54. In 1954 he became Professor of Medieval and Renaissance Literature at Cambridge. He was an outstanding and popular lecturer and had a deep and lasting influence on his pupils.

C. S. Lewis was for many years an atheist, and described his conversion in *Surprised by Joy*: "In the Trinity Term of 1929 I gave in, and admitted that God was God . . . perhaps the most dejected and reluctant convert in all England." It was this experience that helped him to understand not only apathy but active unwillingness to accept religion and, as a Christian writer, gifted with an exceptionally brilliant and logical mind and a lucid, lively style, he was without peer. *The Problem of Pain*, *The Screwtape Letters*, *Mere Christianity*, *The Four Loves* and the posthumous *Letters to Malcolm: Chiefly on Prayer* are only a few of his best-selling works. He also wrote books for children, and some science fiction, besides many works of literary criticism. His works are known to millions of people all over the world in translation. He died on 22nd November 1963, at his home in Oxford.

PREFACE AND ACKNOWLEDGMENTS

C. S. Lewis had finished putting this book together shortly before his death on 22nd November 1963. It is devoted almost entirely to religion and the pieces are derived from various sources. Some of them have appeared in *They Asked for a Paper* (Geoffrey Bles, London 1962, 21s.), a collection whose subjects included literature, ethics and theology. 'Screwtape Proposes a Toast' was initially published in Great Britain as part of a hard-covered book called *The Screwtape Letters and Screwtape Proposes a Toast* (Geoffrey Bles, London 1961, 12s. 6d.). This consisted of the original 'The Screwtape Letters', together with the 'Toast', and also a new preface by Lewis. Meantime, 'Screwtape Proposes a Toast' had already appeared in the United States, first as an article in *The Saturday Evening Post* and then during 1960 in a hard-covered collection, *The World's Last Night* (Harcourt Brace and World, New York).

In the new preface for *The Screwtape Letters and Screwtape Proposes a Toast*, which we have reprinted in this book, Lewis explains the conception and birth of the 'Toast'. It would be quite wrong to call the address 'another Screwtape letter'. What he described as the technique of 'diabolical ventriloquism' is indeed still there: Screwtape's whites are our blacks and whatever he welcomes we should dread. But, whilst the form still broadly persists, there its affinity to the original *Letters* ends. They were mainly concerned with the moral life of an individual; in the 'Toast' the substance of the quest is now rather the need to respect and foster the mind of the young boy and girl.

'A Slip of the Tongue' (a sermon preached in Magdalene College Chapel) appears in a book for the first time. 'The Inner Ring' was a Memorial Oration delivered at King's College, University of London in 1944; 'Is Theology Poetry?' and 'On Obstinacy in Belief' were both papers read to the Socratic Club, subsequently first appearing in the 'Socratic Digest' in 1944 and 1955 respectively. 'Transposition' is a slightly fuller version of a sermon preached in Mansfield College, Oxford; whilst 'The Weight of Glory' was a sermon given in the Church of St. Mary the Virgin, Oxford, and first published by SPCK. All these five papers were published by kind permission in *They Asked for a Paper*. 'Good Work and Good Works' first appeared in *The Catholic Art Quarterly* and then in *The World's Last Night*.

At the end of his preface to *They Asked for a Paper*, Lewis wrote: 'Since these papers were composed at various times during the last twenty years, passages in them which some readers may find reminiscent of my later work are in fact anticipatory or embryonic. I have allowed myself to be persuaded that such overlaps were not a fatal objection to their republication.' We are delighted that he allowed himself to be persuaded in the same way over this paperback collection of pieces on religious themes.

J.E.G.

CONTENTS

SCREWTAPE PROPOSES A TOAST

I was often asked or advised to add to the original "Screwtape Letters", but for many years I felt not the least inclination to do it. Though I had never written anything more easily, I never wrote with less enjoyment. The ease came, no doubt, from the fact that the device of diabolical letters, once you have thought of it, exploits itself spontaneously, like Swift's big and little men, or the medical and ethical philosophy of "Erewhon", as Anstey's Garuda Stone. It would run away with you for a thousand pages if you gave it its head. But though it was easy to twist one's mind into the diabolical attitude, it was not fun, or not for long. The strain produced a sort of spiritual cramp. The world into which I had to project myself while I spoke through Screwtape was all dust, grit, thirst and itch. Every trace of beauty, freshness and geniality had to be excluded. It almost smothered me before I was done. It would have smothered my readers if I had prolonged it.

I had, moreover, a sort of grudge against my book for not being a different book which no one could write. Ideally, Screwtape's advice to Wormwood should have been balanced by archangelical advice to the patient's guardian angel. Without this the picture of human life is lop-sided. But who could supply the deficiency? Even if a man—and he would have to be a far better man than I—could scale the spiritual heights required, what "answerable style" could he use? For the style would really be part of the content. Mere advice would be no *good; every sentence would have to smell of Heaven. And nowadays even if you could write prose like Traherne's, you wouldn't be allowed to, for the canon of " functionalism " has disabled literature for half its functions. (At bottom, every ideal of style dictates not only how we should say things but what sort of things we may say.)*

Then, as years went on and the stifling experience of writing the " Letters " became a weaker memory, reflections on this and that which seemed somehow to demand Screwtapian treatment began to occur to me. I was resolved never to write another " Letter ". The idea of something like a lecture or " address " hovered vaguely in my mind, now forgotten, now recalled, never written. Then came an invitation from The Saturday Evening Post, and that pressed the trigger.

C.S.L.

THE SCENE is in Hell at the annual dinner of the Tempters' Training College for young Devils. The Principal, Dr. Slubgob, has just proposed the health of the guests. Screwtape, who is the guest of honour, rises to reply:

Mr. Principal, your Imminence, your Disgraces, my Thorns, Shadies, and Gentledevils: It is customary on these occasions for the speaker to address himself chiefly to those among you who have just graduated and who will very soon be posted to official Temperships on Earth. It is a custom I willingly obey. I well remember with what trepidation I awaited my own first appointment. I hope, and believe, that each one of you has the same uneasiness to-night. Your career is before you.

Hell expects and demands that it should be—as Mine was—one of unbroken success. If it is not, you know what awaits you.

I have no wish to reduce the wholesome and realistic element of terror, the unremitting anxiety, which must act as the lash and spur to your endeavours. How often you will envy the humans their faculty of sleep! Yet at the same time I would wish to put before you a moderately encouraging view of the strategical situation as a whole.

Your dreaded Principal has included in a speech full of points something like an apology for the banquet which he has set before us. Well, gentledevils, no one blames *him*. But it would be vain to deny that the human souls on whose anguish we have been feasting to-night were of pretty poor quality. Not all the most skilful cookery of our tormentors could make them better than insipid.

Oh to get one's teeth again into a Farinara, a Henry VIII, or even a Hitler! There was real crackling there; something to crunch; a rage, an egotism, a cruelty only just less robust than our own. It put up a delicious resistance to being devoured. It warmed your innards when you'd got it down.

Instead of this, what have we had to-night? There was a municipal authority with Graft sauce. But personally I could not detect in him the flavour of a really passionate and brutal avarice such as delighted one in the great tycoons of the last century. Was he not unmistakably a Little Man—a creature of the petty rake-off pocketed with a petty joke in private and denied with the stalest platitudes in his public utterances—a grubby little nonentity who had drifted into corruption, only just realising that he was corrupt, and chiefly because everyone else did it? Then there was the lukewarm Casserole of Adulterers. Could you find in it any trace of a fully inflamed, defiant, rebellious, insatiable lust? I couldn't. They all tasted to me like under-sexed morons who had blundered or trickled into the wrong beds in automatic response to sexy advertisements, or to make themselves feel modern and emancipated, or to reassure themselves about their virility or their "normalcy", or even because they had nothing else to do. Frankly, to me who have tasted Messalina and Casanova, they were nauseating. The Trade Unionist garnished with Claptrap was perhaps a shade better. He had done some real harm. He had, not quite unknowingly, worked for bloodshed, famine, and the extinction of liberty. Yes, in a way. But what a way! He thought of those ultimate objectives so little. Toeing the party line, self-importance, and above all mere routine, were what really dominated his life.

But now comes the point. Gastronomically, all this is deplorable. But I hope none of us puts gastronomy first. Is it not, in another and far more serious way, full of hope and promise?

Consider, first, the mere quantity. The quality may be wretched; but we never had souls (of a sort) in more abundance.

And then the triumph. We are tempted to say that such souls—or such residual puddles of what once was soul—are hardly worth damning. Yes, but the Enemy (for whatever inscrutable and perverse reason) thought them worth trying to save. Believe me, he did. You youngsters who have not yet been on active service have no idea with what labour, with what delicate skill, each of these miserable creatures was finally captured.

The difficulty lay in their very smallness and flabbiness. Here were vermin so muddled in mind, so passively responsive to environment, that it was very hard to raise them to that level of clarity and deliberateness at which mortal sin becomes possible. To raise them just enough; but not that fatal millimetre of "too much". For then, of course, all would possibly have been lost. They might have seen; they might have repented. On the other hand, if they had been raised too little, they would very possibly have qualified for Limbo, as creatures suitable neither for Heaven nor for Hell; things that, having failed to make the grade, are allowed to sink into a more or less contented sub-humanity forever.

In each individual choice of what the Enemy would call the "wrong" turning such creatures are at first hardly, if at all, in a state of full spiritual responsibility. They do not understand either the source or the real character of the prohibitions they are breaking. Their consciousness hardly exists apart from the social atmosphere that surrounds them. And of course we have contrived that their very language should be all smudge and blur; what would be a *bribe* in someone else's profession is a *tip* or a *present* in theirs. The first job of their Tempters was to harden these choices of the Hell-ward roads into a habit by steady repetition. But then (and this was all-important) to turn the habit into a principle —a principle the creature is prepared to defend. After that, all will go well. Conformity to the social environment, at first merely instinctive or even mechanical— how should a *jelly* not conform?—now becomes an unacknowledged creed or ideal of Togetherness or Being like Folks. Mere ignorance of the law they break now turns into a vague theory about it—remember they know no history—a theory expressed by calling it *conventional* or *puritan* or *bourgeois* "morality". Thus gradually there comes to exist at the centre of the creature a hard, tight, settled core of resolution to go on being what it is, and even to resist moods that might tend to alter it. It is a very small core; not at all reflective (they are too ignorant) nor defiant (their emotional and imaginative poverty excludes that); almost, in its own way, prim and demure; like a pebble, or a very young cancer. But it will serve our turn. Here at last is a real and deliberate, though not fully articulate, rejection of what the Enemy calls Grace.

These, then, are two welcome phenomena. First, the abundance of our captures; however tasteless our fare, we are in no danger of famine. And secondly, the triumph; the skill of our Tempters has never stood higher. But the third moral, which I have not yet drawn, is the most important of all.

The sort of souls on whose despair and ruin we have—well, I won't say feasted, but at any rate subsisted—to-night are increasing in numbers and will continue to increase. Our advices from Lower Command assure us that this is so; our directives warn us to orient all our tactics in view of this situation. The "great" sinners, those in whom vivid and genial passions have been pushed beyond the bounds and in whom an immense concentration of will has been devoted to objects which the Enemy abhors, will not disappear. But they will grow rarer. Our catches will be ever more numerous; but they will consist increasingly of trash—trash which we should once have thrown to Cerberus and the hellhounds as unfit for diabolical consumption. And there are two things I want you to understand about this. First, that however depressing it may seem, it is really a change for the better. And secondly, I would draw your attention to the means by which it has been brought about.

It is a change for the better. The great (and toothsome) sinners are made out of the very same material as those horrible phenomena, the great Saints. The virtual disappearance of such material may mean insipid meals for us. But is it not utter frustration and famine for the Enemy? He did not create the humans—He did not become one of them and die among them by torture—in order to produce candidates for Limbo; "failed" humans. He wanted to make Saints; gods; things like Himself. Is the dullness of your present fare not a very small price to pay for the delicious knowledge that His whole great experiment is petering out? But not only that. As the great sinners grow fewer, and the majority lose all individuality, the great sinners become far more effective agents for us. Every dictator or even demagogue —almost every film-star or crooner—can now draw tens of thousands of the human sheep with him. They give themselves (what there is of them) to him; in him, to us. There may come a time when we shall have no need to bother about *individual* temptation at all, except for the few. Catch the bell-wether and his whole flock comes after him.

But do you realise how we have succeeded in reducing so many of the human race to the level of ciphers? This has not come about by accident. It has been our answer —and a magnificent answer it is—to one of the most serious challenges we ever had to face.

Let me recall to your minds what the human situation was in the latter half of the nineteenth century—the period at which I ceased to be a practising Tempter and was rewarded with an administrative post. The great movement towards liberty and equality among men had by then borne solid fruit and grown mature. Slavery had been abolished. The American War of Independence had been won. The French Revolution had succeeded. Religious toleration was almost everywhere on the increase. In that movement there had originally been many elements which were in our favour. Much Atheism, much Anti-Clericalism, much envy and thirst for revenge, even some (rather absurd) attempts to revive Paganism, were mixed in it. It was not easy to determine what our own attitude should be. On the one hand it was a bitter blow to us—it still is—that any sort of men who had been hungry should be fed or any who had long worn chains should have them struck off. But on the other hand, there was in the movement so much rejection of faith, so much materialism, secularism, and hatred, that we felt we were bound to encourage it.

But by the latter part of the century the situation was much simpler, and also much more ominous. In the English sector (where I saw most of my front-line service) a horrible thing had happened. The Enemy, with His usual sleight of hand, had largely appropriated this progressive or liberalising movement and perverted it to His own ends. Very little of its old anti-Christianity remained. The dangerous phenomenon called Christian Socialism was rampant. Factory owners of the good old type who grew rich on sweated labour, instead of being assassinated by their workpeople—we could have used that—were being frowned upon by their own class. The rich were increasingly giving up their powers not in the face of revolution and compulsion, but in obedience to their own consciences. As for the poor who benefited by this, they were behaving in a most disappointing fashion. Instead of using their new liberties—as we reasonably hoped and expected—for massacre, rape, and looting, or even for perpetual intoxication, they were perversely engaged in becoming cleaner, more orderly, more thrifty, better educated, and even more virtuous. Believe me, gentledevils, the threat of something like a really healthy state of society seemed then perfectly serious.

Thanks to our Father Below the threat was averted. Our counter-attack was on two levels. On the deepest level our dealers contrived to call into full life an element which had been implicit in the movement from its earliest days. Hidden in the heart of this striving for Liberty there was also a deep hatred of personal freedom. That invaluable man Rousseau first revealed it. In his perfect democracy, you remember, only the state religion is permitted, slavery is restored, and the individual is told that he has really willed (though he didn't know it) whatever the Government tells him to do. From that starting point, *via* Hegel (another indispensable propagandist on our side) we easily contrived both the Nazi and the Communist state. Even in England we were pretty successful. I heard the other day that in that country a man could not, without a permit, cut down his own tree with his own axe, make it into planks with his own saw, and use the planks to build a tool-shed in his own garden.

Such was our counter-attack on one level. You, who are mere beginners, will not be entrusted with work of that kind. You will be attached as Tempters to private persons. Against them, or through them, our counter-attack takes a different form.

Democracy is the word with which you must lead them by the nose. The good work which our philological experts have already done in the corruption of human language makes it unnecessary to warn you that they should never be allowed to give this word a clear and definable meaning. They won't. It will never occur to them that *Democracy* is properly the name of a political system, even a system of voting, and that this has only the most remote and tenuous connection with what you are trying to sell them. Nor, of course, must they ever be allowed to raise Aristotle's question: whether " democratic behaviour " means the behaviour that democracies like or the behaviour that will preserve a democracy. For if they did, it could hardly fail to occur to them that these need not be the same.

You are to use the word purely as an incantation; if you like, purely for its selling power. It is a name they venerate. And of course it is connected with the political ideal that men should be equally treated. You then make a stealthy transition in their minds from this political ideal to a factual belief that all men *are* equal. Especially the man you are working on. As a result you can use the word *Democracy* to sanction in his thought the most degrading (and also the least enjoyable) of all human feelings. You can get him to practise, not only without shame but with a positive glow of self-approval, conduct which, if undefended by the magic word, would be universally derided.

The feeling I mean is of course that which prompts a man to say *I'm as good as you.*

The first and most obvious advantage is that you thus induce him to enthrone at the centre of his life a good, solid resounding lie. I don't mean merely that his statement is false in fact, that he is no more equal to everyone he meets in kindness, honesty, and good sense than in height or waist-measurement. I mean that he does not believe it himself. No man who says *I'm as good as you* believes it. He would not say it if he did. The St. Bernard never says it to the toy dog, nor the scholar to the dunce, nor the employable to the bum, nor the pretty woman to the plain. The claim to equality, outside the strictly political field, is made only by those who feel themselves to be in some way inferior. What it expresses is precisely the itching, smarting, writhing awareness of an inferiority which the patient refuses to accept.

And therefore resents. Yes, and therefore resents every kind of superiority in others; denigrates it; wishes its annihilation. Presently he suspects every mere difference of being a claim to superiority. No one must be different from himself in voice, clothes, manners, recreations, choice of food. " Here is someone who speaks English rather more clearly and euphoniously than I—it must be a vile, upstage, lah-di-dah affectation. Here's a fellow who says he doesn't like hot dogs—thinks himself too good for them no doubt. Here's a man who hasn't turned on the jukebox—he must be one of those highbrows and is doing it to show off. If they were the right sort of chaps they'd be like me. They've no business to be different. It's undemocratic."

Now this useful phenomenon is in itself by no means new. Under the name of Envy it has been known to the humans for thousands of years. But hitherto they always regarded it as the most odious, and also the most comical, of vices. Those who were aware of feeling it felt it with shame; those who were not gave it no quarter in others. The delightful novelty of the present situation is that you can sanction it—make it respectable and even laudable— by the incantatory use of the word *democratic*.

Under the influence of this incantation those who are

in any or every way inferior can labour more whole-heartedly and successfully than ever before to pull down everyone else to their own level. But that is not all. Under the same influence, those who come, or could come, nearer to a full humanity, actually draw back from it for fear of being *undemocratic*. I am credibly informed that young humans now sometimes suppress an incipient taste for classical music or good literature because it might prevent their Being like Folks; that people who would really wish to be—and are offered the Grace which would enable them to be—honest, chaste, or temperate, refuse it. To accept might make them Different, might offend again the Way of Life, take them out of Togetherness, impair their Integration with the Group. They might (horror of horrors!) become individuals.

All is summed up in the prayer which a young female human is said to have uttered recently : " Oh God, make me a normal twentieth-century girl!" Thanks to our labours, this will mean increasingly, " Make me a minx, a moron, and a parasite."

Meanwhile, as a delightful by-product, the few (fewer every day) who will not be made Normal and Regular and Like Folks and Integrated, increasingly tend to become in reality the prigs and cranks which the rabble would in any case have believed them to be. For suspicion often creates what it suspects. ("Since, whatever I do, the neighbours are going to think me a witch, or a Communist agent, I might as well be hanged for a sheep as a lamb and become one in reality.") As a result we now have an intelligentsia which, though very small, is very useful to the cause of Hell.

But that is a mere by-product. What I want to fix your attention on is the vast, over-all movement towards the discrediting, and finally the elimination, of every kind of human excellence—moral, cultural, social, or intellectual. And is it not pretty to notice how *Democracy* (in the incantatory sense) is now doing for us the work that was once done by the most ancient Dictatorships, and by the same methods? You remember how one of the Greek Dictators (they called them " tyrants " then) sent an envoy to another Dictator to ask his advice about the principles of government. The second Dictator led the envoy into a field of corn, and there he snicked off with his cane the top of every stalk that rose an inch or so above the general level. The moral was plain. Allow no pre-eminence among your subjects. Let no man live who is wiser, or better, or more famous, or even handsomer than the mass. Cut them all down to a level; all slaves, all ciphers, all nobodies. All equals. Thus Tyrants could practise, in a sense, " democracy." But now " democracy " can do the same work without any other tyranny than her own. No one need now go through the field with a cane. The little stalks will now of themselves bite the tops off the big ones. The big ones are beginning to bite off their own in their desire to Be Like Stalks.

I have said that to secure the damnation of these little souls, these creatures that have almost ceased to be individual, is a laborious and tricky work. But if proper pains and skill are expended, you can be fairly confident of the result. The great sinners *seem* easier to catch. But then they are incalculable. After you have played them for seventy years, the Enemy may snatch them from your claws in the seventy-first. They are capable, you see, of real repentance. They are conscious of real guilt. They are, if things take the wrong turn, as ready to defy the social pressures around them for the Enemy's sake as they were to defy them for ours. It is in some ways more troublesome to track and swat an evasive wasp than to shoot, at close range, a wild elephant. But the elephant is more troublesome if you miss.

My own experience, as I have said, was mainly on the English sector, and I still get more news from it than from any other. It may be that what I am now going to say will not apply so fully to the sectors in which some of you may be operating. But you can make the necessary adjustments when you get there. Some application it will almost certainly have. If it has too little, you must labour to make the country you are dealing with more like what England already is.

In that promising land the spirit of *I'm as good as you* has already become something more than a generally social influence. It begins to work itself into their educational system. How far its operations there have gone at the present moment, I would not like to say with certainty. Nor does it matter. Once you have grasped the tendency, you can easily predict its future developments; especially as we ourselves will play our part in the developing. The basic principle of the new education is to be that dunces and idlers must not be made to feel inferior to intelligent and industrious pupils. That would be "undemocratic". These differences between the pupils —for they are obviously and nakedly *individual* differences—must be disguised. This can be done on various levels. At universities, examinations must be framed so that nearly all the students get good marks. Entrance examinations must be framed so that all, or nearly all, citizens can go to universities, whether they have any power (or wish) to profit by higher education or not. At schools, the children who are too stupid or lazy to learn languages and mathematics and elementary science can be set to doing the things that children used to do in their spare time. Let them, for example, make mud-pies and call it modelling. But all the time there must be no faintest hint that they are inferior to the children who are at work. Whatever nonsense they are engaged in must have —I believe the English already use the phrase—" parity of esteem ". An even more drastic scheme is not impossible. Children who are fit to proceed to a higher class may be artificially kept back, because the others would get a *trauma*—Beelzebub, what a useful word!—by being left behind. The bright pupil thus remains democratically fettered to his own age-group throughout his school career, and a boy who would be capable of tackling Aeschylus or Dante sits listening to his coaeval's attempts to spell out A CAT SAT ON THE MAT.

In a word, we may reasonably hope for the virtual abolition of education when *I'm as good as you* has fully had its way. All incentives to learn and all penalties for not learning will vanish. The few who might want to learn will be prevented; who are they to overtop their fellows? And anyway the teachers—or should I say, nurses?—will be far too busy reassuring the dunces and patting them on the back to waste any time on real teaching. We shall no longer have to plan and toil to spread imperturbable conceit and incurable ignorance among men. The little vermin themselves will do it for us.

Of course this would not follow unless all education became state education. But it will. That is part of the same movement. Penal taxes, designed for that purpose, are liquidating the Middle Class, the class who were prepared to save and spend and make sacrifices in order to have their children privately educated. The removal of this class, besides linking up with the abolition of education, is, fortunately, an inevitable effect of the spirit that says *I'm as good as you*. This was, after all, the social group which gave to the humans the overwhelming majority of their scientists, physicians, philosophers, theologians, poets, artists, composers, architects, jurists, and administrators. If ever there was a bunch of tall stalks that needed their tops knocked off, it was surely they. As an English politician remarked not long ago, " A democracy does not want great men."

It would be idle to ask of such a creature whether by *want* it means " need " or " like ". But you had better be clear. For here Aristotle's question comes up again.

We, in Hell, would welcome the disappearance of Democracy in the strict sense of that word; the political arrangement so called. Like all forms of government it often works to our advantage; but on the whole less often than other forms. And what we must realise is that " democracy " in the dialobical sense (*I'm as good as you, Being like Folks, Togetherness*) is the finest instrument we could possibly have for extirpating political Democracies from the face of the earth.

For " democracy " or the " democratic spirit " (diabolical sense) leads to a nation without great men, a nation mainly of subliterates, morally flaccid from lack of discipline in youth, full of the cocksureness which flattery breeds on ignorance, and soft from lifelong pampering. And that is what Hell wishes every democratic people to be. For when such a nation meets in conflict a nation where children have been made to work at school, where talent is placed in high posts, and where the ignorant mass are allowed no say at all in public affairs, only one result is possible.

One Democracy was surprised lately when it found that Russia had got ahead of it in science. What a delicious specimen of human blindness! If the whole tendency of their society is opposed to every sort of excellence, why did they expect their scientists to excel?

It is our function to encourage the behaviour, the manners, the whole attitude of mind, which democracies naturally like and enjoy, because these are the very things which, if unchecked, will destroy democracy. You would almost wonder that even humans don't see it themselves. Even if they don't read Aristotle (that would be undemocratic) you would have thought the French Revolution would have taught them that the behaviour aristocrats naturally like is not the behaviour that preserves aristocracy. They might then have applied the same principle to all forms of government.

But I would not end on that note. I would not—Hell forbid!—encourage in your own minds that delusion which you must carefully foster in the minds of your human victims. I mean the delusion that the fate of nations is *in itself* more important than that of individual souls. The overthrow of free peoples and the multiplication of slave-states are for us a means (besides, of course, being fun); but the real end is the destruction of individuals. For only individuals can be saved or damned, can become sons of the Enemy or food for us. The ultimate value, for us, of any revolution, war, or famine lies in the individual anguish, treachery, hatred, rage, and despair which it may produce. *I'm as good as you* is a useful means for the destruction of democratic societies. But it has a far deeper value as an end in itself, as a state of mind, which necessarily excluding humility, charity, contentment, and all the pleasures of gratitude or admiration, turns a human being away from almost every road which might finally lead him to Heaven.

But now for the pleasantest part of my duty. It falls to my lot to propose on behalf of the guests the health of Principal Slubgob and the Tempters' Training College. Fill your glasses. What is this I see? What is this delicious bouquet I inhale? Can it be? Mr. Principal, I unsay all my hard words about the dinner. I see, and smell, that even under wartime conditions the College cellar still has a few dozen of sound old vintage *Pharisee*. Well, well, well. This is like old times. Hold it beneath your nostrils for a moment, gentledevils. Hold it up to the light. Look at those fiery streaks that writhe and tangle in its dark heart, as if they were contending. And so they are. You know how this wine is blended? Different types of Pharisee have been harvested, trodden, and fermented together to produce its subtle flavour. Types that were most antagonistic to one another on earth. Some were all rules and relics and rosaries; others were all drab clothes, long faces, and petty traditional abstinences from wine or cards or the theatre. Both had in common their self-righteousness and the almost infinite distance between their actual outlook and anything the Enemy really is or commands. The wickedness of other religions was the really live doctrine in the religion of each; slander was its gospel and denigration its litany. How they hated each other up there where the sun shone! How much more they hate each other now that they are forever conjoined but not reconciled. Their astonishment, their resentment, at the combination, the festering of their eternally impenitent spite, passing into our spiritual digestion, will work like fire. Dark fire. All said and done, my friends, it will be an ill day for us if what most humans mean by "religion" ever vanishes from the Earth. It can still send us the truly delicious sins. The fine flower of unholiness can grow only in the close neighbourhood of the Holy. Nowhere do we tempt so successfully as on the very steps of the altar.

Your Imminence, your Disgraces, my Thorns, Shadies, and Gentledevils: I give you the toast of—Principal Slubgob and the College!

THE INNER RING

May I read you a few lines from Tolstoi's *War and Peace*?

When Boris entered the room, Prince Andrey was listening to an old general, wearing his decorations, who was reporting something to Prince Andrey, with an expression of soldierly servility on his purple face. " Alright. Please wait ! " he said to the general, speaking in Russian with the French accent which he used when he spoke with contempt. The moment he noticed Boris he stopped listening to the general who trotted imploringly after him and begged to be heard, while Prince Andrey turned to Boris with a cheerful smile and a nod of the head. Boris now clearly understood—what he had already guessed—that side by side with the system of discipline and subordination which were laid down in the Army Regulations, there existed a different and a more real system—the system which compelled a tightly laced general with a purple face to wait respectfully for his turn while a mere captain like Prince Andrey chatted with a mere second lieutenant like Boris. Boris decided at once that he would be guided not by the official system but by this other unwritten system.[1]

When you invite a middle-aged moralist to address you, I suppose I must conclude, however unlikely the conclusion seems, that you have a taste for middle-aged

[1] Part III, chapter 9.

moralising. I shall do my best to gratify it. I shall in fact give you advice about the world in which you are going to live. I do not mean by this that I am going to attempt a talk on what are called current affairs. You probably know quite as much about them as I do. I am not going to tell you—except in a form so general that you will hardly recognise it—what part you ought to play in post-war reconstruction. It is not, in fact, very likely that any of you will be able, in the next ten years, to make any direct contribution to the peace or prosperity of Europe. You will be busy finding jobs, getting married, acquiring facts. I am going to do something more old-fashioned than you perhaps expected. I am going to give advice. I am going to issue warnings. Advice and warnings about things which are so perennial that no one calls them " current affairs ".

And of course everyone knows what a middle-aged moralist of my type warns his juniors against. He warns them against the World, the Flesh, and the Devil. But one of this trio will be enough to deal with to-day. The Devil, I shall leave strictly alone. The association between him and me in the public mind has already gone quite as deep as I wish : in some quarters it has already reached the level of confusion, if not of identification. I begin to realise the truth of the old proverb that he who sups with that formidable host needs a long spoon. As for the Flesh, you must be very abnormal young people if you do not know quite as much about it as I do. But on the World I think I have something to say.

In the passage I have just read from Tolstoi, the young second lieutenant Boris Dubretskoi discovers that there exist in the army two different systems or hierarchies. The one is printed in some little red book and anyone can easily read it up. It also remains constant. A general is always superior to a colonel and a colonel to a captain. The other is not printed anywhere. Nor is it even a formally organised secret society with officers and rules which you would be told after you had been admitted. You are never formally and explicitly admitted by any-one. You discover gradually, in almost indefinable ways, that it exists and that you are outside it; and then later, perhaps, that you are inside it. There are what corres-pond to passwords, but they too are spontaneous and informal. A particular slang, the use of particular nick-names, an allusive manner of conversation, are the marks. But it is not constant. It is not easy, even at a given moment, to say who is inside and who is outside. Some people are obviously in and some are obviously out, but there are always several on the border-line. And if you come back to the same Divisional Headquarters, or Brigade Headquarters, or the same regiment or even the same company, after six weeks' absence, you may find this second hierarchy quite altered. There are no formal admissions or expulsions. People think they are in it after they have in fact been pushed out of it, or before they have been allowed in: this provides great amuse-ment for those who are really inside. It has no fixed name. The only certain rule is that the insiders and out-siders call it by different names. From inside it may be designated, in simple cases, by mere enumeration: it may be called " You and Tony and me ". When it is very secure and comparatively stable in membership it calls itself " we ". When it has to be suddenly expanded to meet a particular emergency it calls itself " All the sensible people at this place ". From outside, if you have despaired of getting into it, you call it " That gang " or

"They" or "So-and-so and his set" or "the Caucus" or "the Inner Ring". If you are a candidate for admission you probably don't call it anything. To discuss it with the other outsiders would make you feel outside yourself. And to mention it in talking to the man who is inside, and who may help you in if this present conversation goes well, would be madness.

Badly as I may have described it, I hope you will all have recognised the thing I am describing. Not, of course, that you have been in the Russian Army or perhaps in any army. But you have met the phenomenon of an Inner Ring. You discovered one in your house at school before the end of the first term. And when you had climbed up to somewhere near it by the end of your second year, perhaps you discovered that within the Ring there was a Ring yet more inner, which in its turn was the fringe of the great school Ring to which the house Rings were only satellites. It is even possible that the School Ring was almost in touch with a Masters' Ring. You were beginning, in fact, to pierce through the skins of the onion. And here, too, at your university—shall I be wrong in assuming that at this very moment, invisible to me, there are several rings—independent systems or concentric rings—present in this room? And I can assure you that in whatever hospital, inn of court, diocese, school, business, or college you arrive after going down, you will find the Rings—what Tolstoi calls the second or unwritten systems.

All this is rather obvious. I wonder whether you will say the same of my next step, which is this. I believe that in all men's lives at certain periods, and in many men's lives at all periods between infancy and extreme old age, one of the most dominant elements is the desire to be

inside the local Ring and the terror of being left outside.
This desire, in one of its forms, has indeed had ample
justice done to it in literature. I mean, in the form of
snobbery. Victorian fiction is full of characters who are
hag-ridden by the desire to get inside that particular
Ring which is, or was, called Society. But it must be
clearly understood that " Society ", in that sense of the
word, is merely one of a hundred Rings and snobbery
therefore only one form of the longing to be inside.
People who believe themselves to be free, and indeed are
free, from snobbery, and who read satires on snobbery
with tranquil superiority, may be devoured by the desire
in another form. It may be the very intensity of their
desire to enter some quite different Ring which renders
them immune from the allurements of high life. An invitation from a duchess would be very cold comfort to a
man smarting under the sense of exclusion from some
artistic or communist côterie. Poor man—it is not large,
lighted rooms, or champagne, or even scandals about
peers and Cabinet Ministers that he wants: it is the
sacred little attic or studio, the heads bent together, the
fog of tobacco smoke, and the delicious knowledge that
we—we four or five all huddled beside this stove—are
the people who *know*. Often the desire conceals itself so
well that we hardly recognise the pleasures of fruition.
Men tell not only their wives but themselves that it is a
hardship to stay late at the office or the school on some
bit of important extra work which they have been let in
for because they and So-and-so and the two others are
the only people left in the place who really know how
things are run. But it is not quite true. It is a terrible
bore, of course, when old Fatty Smithson draws you aside
and whispers " Look here, we've got to get you in on

this examination somehow " or " Charles and I saw at once that you've got to be on this committee." A terrible bore . . . ah, but how much more terrible if you were left out! It is tiring and unhealthy to lose your Saturday afternoons : but to have them free because you don't matter, that is much worse.

Freud would say, no doubt, that the whole thing is a subterfuge of the sexual impulse. I wonder whether the shoe is not sometimes on the other foot, I wonder whether, in ages of promiscuity, many a virginity has not been lost less in obedience to Venus than in obedience to the lure of the caucus. For of course, when promiscuity is the fashion, the chaste are outsiders. They are ignorant of something that other people know. They are uninitiated. And as for lighter matters, the numbers who first smoked or first got drunk for a similar reason is probably very large.

I must now make a distinction. I am not going to say that the existence of Inner Rings is an evil. It is certainly unavoidable. There must be confidential discussions : and it is not only not a bad thing, it is (in itself) a good thing, that personal friendship should grow up between those who work together. And it is perhaps impossible that the official hierarchy of any organisation should quite coincide with its actual workings. If the wisest and most energetic people invariably held the highest posts, it might coincide; since they often do not, there must be people in high positions who are really deadweights and people in lower positions who are more important than their rank and seniority would lead you to suppose. In that way the second, unwritten system is bound to grow up. It is necessary; and perhaps it is not a necessary evil. But the desire which draws us into Inner Rings is another matter. A thing may be morally neutral and yet the desire for that thing may be dangerous. As Byron has said :

> Sweet is a legacy, and passing sweet
> The unexpected death of some old lady.

The painless death of a pious relative at an advanced age is not an evil. But an earnest desire for her death on the part of her heirs is not reckoned a proper feeling, and the law frowns on even the gentlest attempt to expedite her departure. Let Inner Rings be an unavoidable and even an innocent feature of life, though certainly not a beautiful one; but what of our longing to enter them, our anguish when we are excluded, and the kind of pleasure we feel when we get in?

I have no right to make assumptions about the degree to which any of you may already be compromised. I must not assume that you have ever first neglected, and finally shaken off, friends whom you really loved and who might have lasted you a lifetime, in order to court the friendship of those who appeared to you more important, more esoteric. I must not ask whether you have ever derived actual pleasure from the loneliness and humiliation of the outsiders after you yourself were in : whether you have talked to fellow members of the Ring in the presence of outsiders simply in order that the outsiders might envy; whether the means whereby, in your days of probation, you propitiated the Inner Ring, were always wholly admirable. I will ask only one question— and it is, of course a rhetorical question which expects no answer. In the whole of your life as you now remember it, has the desire to be on the right side of that invisible line ever prompted you to any act or word on which, in the cold small hours of a wakeful night, you can look back with satisfaction? If so, your case is more fortunate than most.

But I said I was going to give advice, and advice should deal with the future, not the past. I have hinted at the past only to awake you to what I believe to be the real nature of human life. I don't believe that the economic motive and the erotic motive account for everything that goes on in what we moralists call the World. Even if you add Ambition I think the picture is still incomplete. The lust for the esoteric, the longing to be inside, take many forms which are not easily recognisable as Ambition. We hope, no doubt, for tangible profits from every Inner Ring we penetrate : power, money, liberty to break rules, avoidance of routine duties, evasion of discipline. But all these would not satisfy us if we did not get in addition the delicious sense of secret intimacy. It is no doubt a great convenience to know that we need fear no official reprimands from our official senior because he is old Percy, a fellow-member of our Ring. But we don't value the intimacy only for the sake of convenience; quite equally we value the convenience as a proof of the intimacy.

My main purpose in this address is simply to convince you that this desire is one of the great permanent mainsprings of human action. It is one of the factors which go to make up the world as we know it—this whole pell-mell of struggle, competition, confusion, graft, disappointment and advertisement, and if it is one of the permanent mainsprings then you may be quite sure of this. Unless you take measures to prevent it, this desire is going to be one of the chief motives of your life, from the first day on which you enter your profession until the day when you are too old to care. That will be the natural thing—the life that will come to you of its own accord. Any other kind of life, if you lead it, will be the result of conscious and continuous effort. If you do nothing about it, if you drift with the stream, you will in fact be an "inner ringer". I don't say you'll be a successful one; that's as may be. But whether by pining and moping outside Rings that you can never enter, or by passing triumphantly further and further in—one way or the other you will be that kind of man.

I have already made it fairly clear that I think it better for you not to be that kind of man. But you may have an open mind on the question. I will therefore suggest two reasons for thinking as I do.

It would be polite and charitable, and in view of your age reasonable too, to suppose that none of you is yet a scoundrel. On the other hand, by the mere law of averages (I am saying nothing against free will) it is almost certain that at least two or three of you before you die will have become something very like scoundrels. There must be in this room the makings of at least that number of unscrupulous, treacherous, ruthless egotists. The choice is still before you; and I hope you will not take my hard words about your possible future characters as a token of disrespect to your present characters. And the prophecy I make is this. To nine out of ten of you the choice which could lead to scoundrelism will come, when it does come, in no very dramatic colours. Obviously bad men, obviously threatening or bribing, will almost certainly not appear. Over a drink or a cup of coffee, disguised as a triviality and sandwiched between two jokes, from the lips of a man, or woman, whom you have recently been getting to know rather better and whom you hope to know better still—just at the moment when your are most anxious not to appear crude, or naïf or a prig—the hint will come. It will be the hint of something which is not quite in accordance with the technical rules of fair play : something which the public, the ignorant, romantic public, would never understand : something which even the outsiders in your own profession are apt to make a fuss about : but something, says your new friend, which " we "—and at the word " we " you try not to blush for mere pleasure—something " we always do ". And you will be drawn in, if you are drawn in, not by desire for gain or ease, but simply because at that moment, when the cup was so near your lips, you cannot bear to be thrust back again into the cold outer world. It would be so terrible to see the other man's face —that genial, confidential, delightfully sophisticated face —turn suddenly cold and contemptuous, to know that you had been tried for the Inner Ring and rejected. And then, if you are drawn in, next week it will be something a little further from the rules, and next year something further still, but all in the jolliest, friendliest spirit. It may end in a crash, a scandal, and penal servitude : it may end in millions, a peerage, and giving prizes at your old school. But you will be a scoundrel.

That is my first reason. Of all passions the passion for the Inner Ring is most skilful in making a man who is not yet a very bad man do very bad things.

My second reason is this. The torture allotted to the Danaids in the classical underworld, that of attempting to fill sieves with water, is the symbol not of one vice but of all vices. It is the very mark of a perverse desire that it seeks what is not to be had. The desire to be inside the invisible line illustrates this rule. As long as you are governed by that desire you will never get what you want. You are trying to peel an onion : if you succeed there will be nothing left. Until you conquer the fear of being an outsider, an outsider you will remain.

This is surely very clear when you come to think of it. If you want to be made free of a certain circle for some wholesome reason—if, say, you want to join a musical society because you really like music—then there is a possibility of satisfaction. You may find yourself playing in a quartet and you may enjoy it. But if all you want is to be in the know, your pleasure will be short-lived. The circle cannot have from within the charm it had from outside. By the very act of admitting you it has lost its magic. Once the first novelty is worn off the members of this circle will be no more interesting than your old friends. Why should they be? You were not looking for virtue or kindness or loyalty or humour or learning or wit or any of the things that can be really enjoyed. You merely wanted to be " in ". And that is a pleasure that cannot last. As soon as your new associates have been staled to you by custom, you will be looking for another Ring. The rainbow's end will still be ahead of you. The old Ring will now be only the drab background for your endeavour to enter the new one.

And you will always find them hard to enter, for a reason you very well know. You yourself, once you are in, want to make it hard for the next entrant, just as those who are already in made it hard for you. Naturally. In any wholesome group of people which holds together for a good purpose, the exclusions are in a sense accidental. Three or four people who are together for the sake of some piece of work exclude others because there is work only for so many or because the others can't in fact do it.

Your little musical group limits its numbers because the rooms they meet in are only so big. But your genuine Inner Ring exists for exclusion. There'd be no fun if there were no outsiders. The invisible line would have no meaning unless most people were on the wrong side of it. Exclusion is no accident : it is the essence.

The quest of the Inner Ring will break your hearts unless you break it. But if you break it, a surprising result will follow. If in your working hours you make the work your end, you will presently find yourself all unawares inside the only circle in your profession that really matters. You will be one of the sound craftsmen, and other sound craftsmen will know it. This group of craftsmen will by no means coincide with the Inner Ring or the Important People or the People in the Know. It will not shape that professional policy or work up that professional influence which fights for the profession as a whole against the public : nor will it lead to those periodic scandals and crises which the Inner Ring produces. But it will do those things which that profession exists to do and will in the long run be responsible for all the respect which that profession in fact enjoys and which the speeches and advertisements cannot maintain. And if in your spare time you consort simply with the people you like, you will again find that you have come unawares to a real inside : that you are indeed snug and safe at the centre of something which, seen from without, would look exactly like an Inner Ring. But the difference is that its secrecy is accidental, and its exclusiveness a by-product, and no one was led thither by the lure of the esoteric : for it is only four or five people who like one another meeting to do things that they like. This is friendship. Aristotle placed it among the virtues. It causes perhaps half of all the happiness in the world, and no Inner Ring can ever have it.

We are told in Scripture that those who ask get. That is true, in senses I can't now explore. But in another sense there is much truth in the schoolboy's principle " them as asks shan't have ". To a young person, just entering on adult life, the world seems full of " insides ", full of delightful intimacies and confidentialities, and he desires to enter them. But if he follows that desire he will reach no " inside " that is worth reaching. The true road lies in quite another direction. It is like the house in *Alice Through the Looking Glass.*

Memorial Oration at King's College, London, 1944

IS THEOLOGY POETRY?

The question I have been asked to discuss to-night—" Is Theology Poetry?"—is not of my own choosing. I find myself, in fact, in the position of a candidate at an examination; and I must obey the advice of my tutors by first making sure that I know what the question means.

By Theology we mean, I suppose, the systematic series of statements about God and about man's relation to Him which the believers of a religion make. And in a paper set me by this Club I may perhaps assume that Theology means principally Christian Theology. I am the bolder to make this assumption because something of what I think about other religions will appear in what I have to say. It must also be remembered that only a minority of the religions of the world have a theology. There was no systematic series of statements which the Greeks agreed in believing about Zeus.

The other term, Poetry, is much harder to define, but I believe I can assume the question which my examiners had in mind without a definition. There are certain things which I feel sure they were not asking me. They were not asking me whether Theology is written in verse. They were not asking me whether most theologians are masters of a " simple, sensuous and passionate " style. I believe they meant : " Is Theology *merely* poetry?" This might be expanded : " Does Theology offer us, at best, only that kind of truth which, according to some critics, poetry offers us?" And the first difficulty of answering the question in that form is that we have no general agreement as to what "poetical truth" means, or whether there is really any such thing. It will be best, therefore, to use for this paper a very vague and modest notion of poetry, simply as writing which arouses and in part satisfies the imagination. And I shall take it that the question I am to answer is this : Does Christian Theology owe its attraction to its power of arousing and satisfying our imagination? Are those who believe it mistaking æsthetic enjoyment for intellectual assent, or assenting because they enjoy?

Faced with this question, I naturally turn to inspect the believer whom I know best—myself. And the first fact I discover, or seem to discover, is that for me at any rate, if Theology is Poetry, it is not very good poetry.

Considered as poetry, the doctrine of the Trinity seems to me to fall between two stools. It has neither the monolithic grandeur of strictly Unitarian conceptions, nor the richness of Polytheism. The omnipotence of God is not, to my taste, a poetical advantage. Odin, fighting against enemies who are not his own creatures and who will in fact defeat him in the end, has a heroic appeal which the God of the Christians cannot have. There is also a certain bareness about the Christian picture of the universe. A future state, and orders of superhuman creatures, are held to exist, but only the slightest hints of their nature are offered. Finally, and worst of all, the whole cosmic story though full of tragic elements yet fails of being a tragedy. Christianity offers the attractions neither of optimism nor of pessimism. It represents the life of the universe as being very like the mortal life of men on this planet—" of a mingled yarn, good and ill together ". The majestic simplifications of Pantheism and the tangled wood of Pagan animism both seem to me, in their different ways, more attractive. Christianity just misses the tidiness of the one and the delicious variety of the other. For I take it there are two things the imagination loves to do. It loves to embrace its object completely, to take it in at a single glance and see it as something harmonious, symmetrical and self-explanatory. That is the classical imagination: the Parthenon was built for it. It also loves to lose itself in a labyrinth, to surrender to the inextricable. That is the romantic imagination: the *Orlando Furioso* was written for it. But Christian Theology does not cater very well for either.

If Christianity is only a mythology, then I find the mythology I believe in is not the one I like best. I like Greek mythology much better: Irish better still: Norse best of all.

Having thus inspected myself, I next inquire how far my case is peculiar. It does not seem, certainly, to be unique. It is not at all plain that men's imaginations have always delighted most in those pictures of the supernatural which they believed. From the twelfth to the seventeenth century Europe seems to have taken an unfailing delight in classical mythology. If the numbers and the gusto of pictures and poems were to be the criterion of belief, we should judge that those ages were pagan; which we know to be untrue.

It looks as if the confusion between imaginative enjoyment and intellectual assent, of which Christians are accused, is not nearly so common or so easy as some people suppose. Even children, I believe, rarely suffer from it. It pleases their imagination to pretend that they are bears or horses; but I do not remember that one was ever under the least delusion. May it not even be that there is something in belief which is hostile to perfect imaginative enjoyment? The sensitive, cultured atheist seems at times to enjoy the æsthetic trappings of Christianity in a way which the believer can only envy. The modern poets certainly enjoy the Greek gods in a way of which I find no trace in Greek literature. What mythological scenes in ancient literature can compare for a moment with Keats's *Hyperion*? In a certain sense we spoil a mythology for imaginative purposes by believing in it. Fairies are popular in England because we don't think they exist; they are no fun at all in Arran or Connemara.

But I must beware of going too far. I have suggested that belief spoils a system for the imagination " in a certain sense ". But not in all senses. If I came to believe in fairies I should almost certainly lose the particular kind of pleasure which I now get from them when reading the *Midsummer Night's Dream*. But later on, when the believed fairies had settled down as inhabitants of my real universe and had been fully connected with other parts of my thought, a new pleasure might arise. The contemplation of what we take to be real is always, I think, in tolerably sensitive minds, attended with a certain sort of æsthetic satisfaction—a sort which depends precisely on its supposed reality. There is a dignity and poignancy in the bare fact that a thing exists. Thus, as Balfour pointed out in *Theism and Humanism* (a book too little read) there are many historical facts which we should not applaud for any obvious humour or pathos if we supposed them to be inventions; but once we believe them to be real we have, in addition to our intellectual satisfaction, a certain æsthetic delight in the idea of them. The story of the Trojan War and the story of the Napoleonic Wars both have an æsthetic effect on us. And the effects are different. And this difference does not depend solely on those differences which would make them different as stories if we believed neither. The *kind* of pleasure the Napoleonic Wars give has a certain difference simply because we believe in them. A believed idea *feels* different from an idea that is not believed. And that peculiar flavour of the believed is never, in my experience, without a special sort of imaginative enjoyment. It is therefore quite true that the Christians do enjoy their world picture, æsthetically, once they have accepted it as true. Every man, I believe, enjoys the world picture which he accepts: for the gravity and finality of the actual is itself an æsthetic stimulus. In this sense, Christianity, Life-Force-Worship, Marxism, Freudianism all become " poetries " to their own believers. But this does not mean that their adherents have chosen them for that reason. On the contrary, this kind of poetry is the result, not the cause, of belief. Theology is, in this sense, poetry to me because I believe it: I do not believe it because it is poetry.

The charge that Theology is mere poetry, if it means that Christians believe it because they find it, antecedently to belief, the most poetically attractive of all world pictures, thus seems to me unplausible in the extreme. There may be evidence for such a charge which I do not know of : but such evidence as I do know is against it.

I am not of course maintaining that Theology, even before you believe it, is totally bare of æsthetic value. But I do not find it superior in this respect to most of its rivals. Consider for a few moments the enormous æsthetic claim of its chief contemporary rival—what we may loosely call the Scientific Outlook,[1] the picture of

[1] I am not suggesting that practising scientists believe it as a

Mr. Wells and the rest. Supposing this to be a myth, is it not one of the finest myths which human imagination has yet produced? The play is preceded by the most austere of all preludes : the infinite void, and matter restlessly moving to bring forth it knows not what. Then, by the millionth millionth chance—what tragic irony—the conditions at one point of space and time bubble up into that tiny fermentation which is the beginning of life. Everything seems to be against the infant hero of our drama—just as everything seems against the youngest son or ill-used stepdaughter at the opening of a fairy-tale. But life somehow wins through. With infinite suffering, against all but insuperable obstacles, it spreads, it breeds, it complicates itself : from the amoeba up to the plant, up to the reptile, up to the mammal. We glance briefly at the age of monsters. Dragons prowl the earth, devour one another and die. Then comes the theme of the younger son and the ugly duckling once more. As the weak, tiny spark of life began amidst the huge hostilities of the inanimate, so now again, amidst the beasts that are far larger and stronger than he, there comes forth a little naked, shivering, cowering creature, shuffling, not yet erect, promising nothing : the product of another millionth millionth chance. Yet somehow he thrives. He becomes the Cave Man with his club and his flints, muttering and growling over his enemies' bones, dragging his screaming mate by her hair (I never could quite make out why), tearing his children to pieces in fierce jealousy till one of them is old enough to tear him, cowering

whole. The delightful name " Wellsianity " (which another member invented during the discussion) would have been much better than " the Scientific Outlook ".

before the horrible gods whom he has created in his own image. But these are only growing pains. Wait till the next Act. There he is becoming true Man. He learns to master Nature. Science comes and dissipates the superstitions of his infancy. More and more he becomes the controller of his own fate. Passing hastily over the present (for it is a mere nothing by the time-scale we are using), you follow him on into the future. See him in the last act, though not the last scene, of this great mystery. A race of demigods now rule the planet—and perhaps more than the planet—for eugenics have made certain that only demigods will be born, and psycho-analysis that none of them shall lose or smirch his divinity, and communism that all which divinity requires shall be ready to their hand. Man has ascended his throne. Henceforward he has nothing to do but to practise virtue, to grow in wisdom, to be happy. And now, mark the final stroke of genius. If the myth stopped at that point, it might be a little bathetic. It would lack the highest grandeur of which human imagination is capable. The last scene reverses all. We have the Twilight of the Gods. All this time, silently, unceasingly, out of all reach of human power, Nature, the old enemy, has been steadily gnawing away. The sun will cool—all suns will cool— the whole universe will run down. Life (every form of life) will be banished, without hope of return, from every inch of infinite space. All ends in nothingness, and "universal darkness covers all". The pattern of the myth thus becomes one of the noblest we can conceive. It is the pattern of many Elizabethan tragedies, where the protagonist's career can be represented by a slowly ascending and then rapidly falling curve, with its highest point in Act IV. You see him climbing up and up, then blazing in his bright meridian, then finally overwhelmed in ruin.

Such a world-drama appeals to every part of us. The early struggles of the hero (a theme delightfully doubled, played first by life, and then by man) appeals to our generosity. His future exaltation gives scope to a reasonable optimism; for the tragic close is so very distant that you need not often think of it—we work with millions of years. And the tragic close itself just gives that irony, that grandeur, which calls forth our defiance, and without which all the rest might cloy. There is a beauty in this myth which well deserves better poetic handling than it has yet received : I hope some great genius will yet crystallise it before the incessant stream of philosophic change carries it all away. I am speaking, of course, of the beauty it has whether you believe it or not. There I can speak from experience : for I, who believe less than half of what it tells me about the past, and less than nothing of what it tells me about the future, am deeply moved when I contemplate it. The only other story—unless, indeed, it is an embodiment of the same story—which similarly moves me is the *Nibelung's Ring* (*Enden sah ich die Welt!*)

We cannot, therefore, turn down Theology, simply because it does not avoid being poetical. All world views yield poetry to those who believe them by the mere fact of being believed. And nearly all have certain poetical merits whether you believe them or not. This is what we should expect. Man is a poetical animal and touches nothing which he does not adorn.

There are, however, two other lines of thought which might lead us to call Theology a mere poetry, and these I must now consider. In the first place, it certainly contains elements similar to those which we find in many early, and even savage, religions. And those elements in the early religions may now seem to us to be poetical. The question here is rather complicated. We now regard the death and return of Balder as a poetical idea, a myth. We are invited to infer thence that the death and resurrection of Christ is a poetical idea, a myth. But we are not really starting with the *datum* " Both are poetical " and thence arguing "Therefore both are false ". Part of the poetical aroma which hangs about Balder is, I believe, due to the fact that we have already come to disbelieve in him. So that disbelief, not poetical experience, is the real starting point of the argument. But this is perhaps an over-subtlety, certainly a subtlety, and I will leave it on one side.

What light is really thrown on the truth or falsehood of Christian Theology by the occurrence of similar ideas in Pagan religion? I think the answer was very well given a fortnight ago by Mr. Brown. Supposing, for purposes of argument, that Christianity is true, then it could avoid all coincidence with other religions only on the supposition that all other religions are one hundred per cent erroneous. To which, you remember, Professor Price replied by agreeing with Mr. Brown and saying : " Yes. From these resemblances you may conclude not ' so much the worse for the Christians ' but ' so much the better for the Pagans '." The truth is that the resemblances tell nothing either for or against the truth of Christian Theology. If you start from the assumption that the Theology is false, the resemblances are quite consistent with that assumption. One would expect creatures of the same sort, faced with the same universe, to make the same false guess more than once. But if you start with the assumption that the Theology is true, the resemblances fit in equally well. Theology, while saying that a special illumination has been vouchsafed to Christians and (earlier) to Jews, also says that there is some divine illumination vouchsafed to all men. The Divine light, we are told, "lighteneth every man". We should, therefore, expect to find in the imagination of great Pagan teachers and myth-makers some glimpse of that theme which we believe to be the very plot of the whole cosmic story—the theme of incarnation, death and re-birth. And the differences between the Pagan Christs (Balder, Osiris, etc.) and the Christ Himself is much what we should expect to find. The Pagan stories are all about someone dying and rising, either every year, or else nobody knows where and nobody knows when. The Christian story is about a historical personage, whose execution can be dated pretty accurately, under a named Roman magistrate, and with whom the society that He founded is in a continuous relation down to the present day. It is not the difference between falsehood and truth. It is the difference between a real event on the one hand and dim dreams or premonitions of that same event on the other. It is like watching something come gradually into focus : first it hangs in the clouds of myth and ritual, vast and vague, then it condenses, grows hard and in a sense small, as a historical event in first-century Palestine. This gradual focussing goes on even inside the Christian tradition itself. The earliest stratum of the Old Testament contains many truths in a form which I take to be legendary, or even mythical—hanging in the clouds : but gradually the truth condenses, becomes more and more historical. From things like Noah's Ark or the sun standing still upon Ajalon, you come down to the court memoirs of King David. Finally you reach the New Testament and history reigns supreme, and the Truth is incarnate. And " incarnate " is here more than a metaphor. It is not an accidental resemblance that what, from the point of view of being, is stated in the form " God became Man ", should involve, from the point of view of human knowledge, the statement " Myth became Fact ". The essential meaning of all things came down from the " heaven " of myth to the " earth " of history. In so doing, it partly emptied itself of its glory, as Christ emptied Himself of His glory to be Man. That is the real explanation of the fact that Theology, far from defeating its rivals by a superior poetry is, in a superficial but quite real sense, less poetical than they. That is why the New Testament is, in the same sense, less poetical than the Old. Have you not often felt in Church, if the first lesson is some great passage, that the second lesson is somehow small by comparison—almost, if one might say so, hum-drum? So it is and so it must be. This is the humiliation of myth into fact, of God into Man : what is everywhere and always, imageless and ineffable, only to be glimpsed in dream and symbol and the acted poetry of ritual, becomes small, solid—no bigger than a man who can lie asleep in a rowing boat on the Lake of Galilee. You may say that this, after all, is a still deeper poetry. I will not contradict you. The humiliation leads to a greater glory. But the humiliation of God and the shrinking or condensation of the myth as it becomes fact, are also quite real.

I have just mentioned symbol : and that brings me to the last head under which I will consider the charge of " mere poetry ". Theology certainly shares with poetry the use of metaphorical or symbolical language. The first

Person of the Trinity is not the Father of the Second in a physical sense. The Second Person did not come " down " to earth in the same sense as a parachutist : nor re-ascend into the sky like a balloon : nor did He literally sit at the right hand of the Father. Why, then, does Christianity talk as if all these things did happen? The agnostic thinks that it does so because those who founded it were quite naïvely ignorant and believed all these statements literally; and we later Christians have gone on using the same language through timidity and conservatism. We are often invited, in Professor Price's words, to throw away the shell and retain the kernel.

There are two questions involved here.

1. What did the early Christians believe? Did they believe that God really has a material palace in the sky and that He received His Son in a decorated state chair placed a little to the right of His own—or did they not? The answer is that the alternative we are offering them was probably never present to their minds at all. As soon as it was present, we know quite well which side of the fence they came down. As soon as the issue of Anthropomorphism was explicitly before the Church in, I think, the second century, Anthropomorphism was condemned. The Church knew the answer (that God has no body and therefore couldn't sit in a chair) as soon as it knew the question. But till the question was raised, of course, people believed neither the one answer nor the other. There is no more tiresome error in the history of thought than to try to sort our ancestors on to this or that side of a distinction which was not in their minds at all. You are asking a question to which no answer exists. It is very probable that most (almost certainly not all) of the first generation of Christians never thought of their faith

without anthropomorphic imagery: and that they were not explicitly conscious, as a modern would be, that it *was* mere imagery. But this does not in the least mean that the essence of their belief was concerned with details about a celestial throne room. That was not what they valued, or what they were prepared to die for. Any one of them who went to Alexandria and got a philisophical education would have recognised the imagery at once for what it was, and would not have felt that his belief had been altered in any way that mattered. My mental picture of an Oxford college, before I saw one, was very different from the reality in physical details. But this did not mean that when I came to Oxford I found my general conception of what a college means to have been a delusion. The physical pictures had inevitably accompanied my thinking, but they had never been what I was chiefly interested in, and much of my thinking had been correct in spite of them. What you think is one thing: what you imagine while you are thinking is another.

The earliest Christians were not so much like a man who mistakes the shell for the kernel as like a man carrying a nut which he hasn't yet cracked. The moment it is cracked, he knows which part to throw away. Till then he holds on to the nut: not because he is a fool but because he isn't.

2. We are invited to restate our belief in a form free from metaphor and symbol. The reason why we don't is that we can't. We can, if you like, say "God entered history" instead of saying "God came down to earth". But, of course, "entered" is just as metaphorical as "came down". You have only substituted horizontal or undefined movement for vertical movement. We can make our language duller; we cannot make it less meta-

phorical. We can make the pictures more prosaic; we cannot be less pictorial. Nor are we Christians alone in this disability. Here is a sentence from a celebrated non-Christian writer, Dr. I. A. Richards.[1] "Only that part of the course of a mental event which takes effect through incoming (sensory) impulses or through effects of past sensory impulses can be said to be thereby known. The reservation no doubt involves complications." Dr. Richards does not mean that the part of the course "takes" effect in the literal sense of the word *takes,* nor that it does so *through* a sensory impulse as you could take a parcel *through* a doorway. In the second sentence "The reservation involves complications", he does not mean that an act of defending, or a seat booked in a train, or an American park, really sets about rolling or folding or curling up a set of coilings or rollings up. In other words, all language about things other than phys-ical objects is necessarily metaphorical.

For all these reasons, then, I think (though we knew even before Freud that the heart is deceitful) that those who accept Theology are not necessarily being guided by taste rather than reason. The picture so often painted of Christians huddling together on an ever narrower strip of beach while the incoming tide of "Science" mounts higher and higher, corresponds to nothing in my own experience. That grand myth which I asked you to ad-mire a few minutes ago is not for me a hostile novelty breaking in on my traditional beliefs. On the contrary, that cosmology is what I started from. Deepening dis-trust and final abandonment of it long preceded my con-version to Christianity. Long before I believed Theology to be true I had already decided that the popular scien-

[1] *Principles of Literary Criticism,* chap. XI.

tific picture at any rate was false. One absolutely central inconsistency ruins it; it is the one we touched on a fortnight ago. The whole picture professes to depend on inferences from observed facts. Unless inference is valid, the whole picture disappears. Unless we can be sure that reality in the remotest nebula or the remotest part obeys the thought-laws of the human scientist here and now in his laboratory—in other words, unless Reason is an absolute—all is in ruins. Yet those who ask me to believe this world picture also ask me to believe that Reason is simply the unforeseen and unintended by-product of mindless matter at one stage of its endless and aimless becoming. Here in flat contradiction. They ask me at the same moment to accept a conclusion and to discredit the only testimony on which that conclusion can be based. The difficulty is to me a fatal one; and the fact that when you put it to many scientists, far from having an answer, they seem not even to understand what the difficulty is, assures me that I have not found a mare's nest but detected a radical disease in their whole mode of thought from the very beginning. The man who has once understood the situation is compelled henceforth to regard the scientific cosmology as being, in principle, a myth; though no doubt a great many true particulars have been worked into it.[1]

After that it is hardly worth noticing minor difficulties. Yet these are many and serious. The Bergsonian critique of orthodox Darwinism is not easy to answer. More disquieting still is Professor D. M. S. Watson's defence.

[1] It is not irrelevant, in considering the mythical character of this cosmology to notice that the two great imaginative expressions of it are *earlier* than the evidence: Keats's *Hyperion* and the *Nibelung's Ring* are pre-Darwinian works.

"Evolution itself," he wrote,[1] "is accepted by zoologists not because it has been observed to occur or . . . can be proved by logically coherent evidence to be true, but because the only alternative, special creation, is clearly incredible." Has it come to that? Does the whole vast structure of modern naturalism depend not on positive evidence but simply on an *a priori* metaphysical prejudice? Was it devised not to get in facts but to keep out God? Even, however, if Evolution in the strict biological sense has some better grounds than Professor Watson suggests—and I can't help thinking it must—we should distinguish Evolution in this strict sense from what may be called the universal evolutionism of modern thought. By universal evolutionism I mean the belief that the very formula of universal process is from imperfect to perfect, from small beginnings to great endings, from the rudimentary to the elaborate: the belief which makes people find it natural to think that morality springs from savage taboos, adult sentiment from infantile sexual maladjustments, thought from instinct, mind from matter, organic from inorganic, cosmos from chaos. This is perhaps the deepest habit of mind in the contemporary world. It seems to me immensely unplausible, because it makes the general course of nature so very unlike those parts of nature we can observe. You remember the old puzzle as to whether the owl came from the egg or the egg from the owl. The modern acquiescence or universal evolutionism is a kind of optical illusion, produced by attending exclusively to the owl's emergence from the egg. We are taught from childhood to notice how the perfect oak grows from the acorn and to forget that the

[1] Quoted in *Science and the B.B.C., Nineteenth Century*, April, 1943.

acorn itself was dropped by a perfect oak. We are reminded constantly that the adult human being was an embryo, never that the life of the embryo came from two adult human beings. We love to notice that the express engine of to-day is the descendant of the "Rocket"; we do not equally remember that the "Rocket" springs not from some even more rudimentary engine, but from something much more perfect and complicated than itself—namely, a man of genius. The obviousness or naturalness which most people seem to find in the idea of emergent evolution thus seems to be a pure hallucination.

On these grounds and others like them one is driven to think that whatever else may be true, the popular scientific cosmology at any rate is certainly not. I left that ship not at the call of poetry but because I thought it could not keep afloat. Something like philosophical idealism or Theism must, at the very worst, be less untrue than that. And idealism turned out, when you took it seriously, to be disguised Theism. And once you accepted Theism you could not ignore the claims of Christ. And when you examined them it appeared to me that you could adopt no middle position. Either he was a lunatic or God. And He was not a lunatic.

I was taught at school, when I had done a sum, to "prove my answer". The proof or verification of my Christian answer to the cosmic sum is this. When I accept Theology I may find difficulties, at this point or that, in harmonising it with some particular truths which are imbedded in the mythical cosmology derived from science. But I can get in, or allow for, science as a whole. Granted that Reason is prior to matter and that the light of that primal Reason illuminates finite minds, I can understand how men should come, by observation and inference, to know a lot about the universe they live in. If, on the other hand, I swallow the scientific cosmology as a whole, then not only can I not fit in Christianity, but I cannot even fit in science. If minds are wholly dependent on brains, and brains on bio-chemistry, and bio-chemistry (in the long run) on the meaningless flux of the atoms, I cannot understand how the thought of those minds should have any more significance than the sound of the wind in the trees. And this is to me the final test. This is how I distinguish dreaming and waking. When I am awake I can, in some degree, account for and study my dream. The dragon that pursued me last night can be fitted into my waking world. I know that there are such things as dreams : I know that I had eaten an indigestible dinner : I know that a man of my reading might be expected to dream of dragons. But while in the nightmare I could not have fitted in my waking experience. The waking world is judged more real because it can thus contain the dreaming world : the dreaming world is judged less real because it cannot contain the waking one. For the same reason I am certain that in passing from the scientific point of view to the theological, I have passed from dream to waking. Christian theology can fit in science, art, morality, and the sub-Christian religions. The scientific point of view cannot fit in any of these things, not even science itself. I believe in Christianity as I believe that the Sun has risen not only because I see it but because by it I see everything else.

The Oxford Socratic Club, 1944

ON OBSTINACY IN BELIEF

Papers have more than once been read to the Socratic Club at Oxford in which a contrast was drawn between a supposedly Christian attitude and a supposedly scientific attitude to belief. We have been told that the scientist thinks it his duty to proportion the strength of his belief exactly to the evidence; to believe less as there is less evidence and to withdraw belief altogether when reliable adverse evidence turns up. We have been told that, on the contrary, the Christian regards it as positively praiseworthy to believe without evidence, or in excess of the evidence, or to maintain his belief unmodified in the teeth of steadily increasing evidence against it. Thus a " faith that has stood firm ", which appears to mean a belief immune from all the assaults of reality, is commended.

If this were a fair statement of the case, then the co-existence within the same species of such scientists and such Christians, would be a very staggering phenomenon. The fact that the two classes appear to overlap, as they do, would be quite inexplicable. Certainly all discussion between creatures so different would be hopeless. The purpose of this essay is to show that things are really not quite so bad as that. The sense in which scientists proportion their belief to the evidence and the sense in which Christians do not, both need to be defined more closely. My hope is that when this has been done, though disagreement between the two parties may remain, they

will not be left staring at one another in wholly dumb
and desperate incomprehension.

And first, a word about belief in general. I do not see
that the state of " proportioning belief to evidence " is
anything like so common in the scientific life as has been
claimed. Scientists are mainly concerned not with believing things but with finding things out. And no one, to
the best of my knowledge, uses the word " believe " about
things he has found out. The doctor says he " believes "
a man was poisoned before he has examined the body;
after the examination, he says the man was poisoned. No
one says that he believes the multiplication table. No one
who catches a thief red-handed says he believes that man
was stealing. The scientist, when at work, that is, when
he is a scientist, is labouring to escape from belief and
unbelief into knowledge. Of course he uses hypotheses or
supposals. I do not think these are beliefs. We must look,
then, for the scientist's behaviour about belief not to his
scientific life but to his leisure hours.

In actual modern English usage the verb " believe ",
except for two special usages, generally expresses a very
weak degree of opinion. " Where is Tom?" " Gone to
London, I believe." The speaker would be only mildly
surprised if Tom had not gone to London after all.
" What was the date?" " 430 B.C., I believe." The
speaker means that he is far from sure. It is the same
with the negative if it is put in the form " I believe not ".
(" Is Jones coming up this term?" " I believe not.") But
if the negative is put in a different form it then becomes
one of the special usages I mentioned a moment ago.
This is of course the form " I don't believe it ", or the still
stronger " I don't believe you ". " I don't believe it " is
far stronger on the negative side than " I believe " is on

the positive. " Where is Mrs. Jones?" " Eloped with the butler, I believe." " I don't believe it." This, especially if said with anger, may imply a conviction which in subjective certitude might be hard to distinguish from knowledge by experience. The other special usage is " I believe " as uttered by a Christian. There is no great difficulty in making the hardened materialist understand, however little he approves, the sort of central attitude which this " I believe " expresses. The materialist need only picture himself replying, to some report of a miracle, " I don't believe it ", and then imagine this same degree of conviction on the opposite side. He knows that he cannot, there and then, produce a refutation of the miracle which would have the certainty of mathematical demonstration; but the formal possibility that the miracle might after all have occurred does not really trouble him any more than a fear that water might not be H. and O. Similarly, the Christian does not necessarily claim to have demonstrative proof; but the formal possibility that God might not exist is not necessarily present in the form of the least actual doubt. Of course there are Christians who hold that such demonstrative proof exists, just as there may be materialists who hold that there is demonstrative disproof. But then, whichever of them is right (if either is) while he retained the proof or disproof would be not believing or disbelieving but knowing. We are speaking of belief and disbelief in the strongest degree but not of knowledge. Belief, in this sense, seems to me to be assent to a proposition which we think so overwhelmingly probable that there is a psychological exclusion of doubt, though not a logical exclusion of dispute.

It may be asked whether belief (and of course disbelief) of this sort ever attaches to any but theological propositions. I think that many beliefs approximate to it; that is, many probabilities seem to us so strong that the absence of logical certainty does not induce in us the least shade of doubt. The scientific beliefs of those who are not themselves scientists often have this character, especially among the uneducated. Most of our beliefs about other people are of the same sort. The scientist himself, or he who was a scientist in the laboratory, has beliefs about his wife and friends which he holds, not indeed without evidence, but with more certitude than the evidence, if weighed in the laboratory manner, would justify. Most of my generation had a belief in the reality of the external world and of other people—if you prefer it, a disbelief in solipsism—far in excess of our strongest arguments. It may be true, as they now say, that the whole thing arose from category mistakes and was a pseudo-problem; but then we didn't know that in the twenties. Yet we managed to disbelieve in solipsism all the same.

There is, of course, no question so far of belief without evidence. We must beware of confusion between the way in which a Christian first assents to certain propositions and the way in which he afterwards adheres to them. These must be carefully distinguished. Of the second it is true, in a sense, to say that Christians do recommend a certain discounting of apparent contrary evidence, and I will later attempt to explain why. But so far as I know it is not expected that a man should assent to these propositions in the first place without evidence or in the teeth of the evidence. At any rate, if anyone expects that, I certainly do not. And in fact, the man who accepts Christianity always thinks he has good evidence; whether, like Dante, *fisici e metafisici argomenti,* or historical evidence, or the evidence of religious experience, or authority, or all these together. For of course authority, however we may value it in this or that particular instance, is a kind of evidence. All of our historical beliefs, most of our geographical beliefs, many of our beliefs about matter that concern us in daily life, are accepted on the authority of other human beings, whether we are Christians, Atheists, Scientists, or Men-in-the-Street.

It is not the purpose of this essay to weigh the evidence, of whatever kind, on which Christians base their belief. To do that would be to write a full-dress *apologia*. All that I need do here is to point out that, at the very worst, this evidence cannot be so weak as to warrant the view that all whom it convinces are indifferent to evidence. The history of thought seems to make this quite plain. We know, in fact, that believers are not cut off from unbelievers by any portentous inferiority of intelligence or any perverse refusal to think. Many of them have been people of powerful minds. Many of them have been scientists. We may suppose them to have been mistaken, but we must suppose that their error was at least plausible. We might indeed, conclude that it was, merely from the multitude and diversity of the arguments against it. For there is not one case against religion, but many. Some say, like Capaneus in Statius, that it is a projection of our primitive fears, *primus in orbe deos fecit timor*: others, with Euhemerus, that it is all a " plant " put up by wicked kings, priests, or capitalists; others, with Tylor, that it comes from dreams about the dead; others, with Frazer, that it is a by-product of agriculture; others, like Freud, that it is a complex; the moderns that it is a category mistake. I will never believe that an error against which so many and various defensive weapons have been found necessary was, from the outset, wholly lacking in plausibility. All this " post haste and rummage in the land " obviously implies a respectable enemy.

There are of course people in our own day to whom the whole situation seems altered by the doctrine of the concealed wish. They will admit that men, otherwise apparently rational, have been deceived by the arguments for religion. But they will say that they have been deceived first by their own desires and produced the arguments afterwards as a rationalisation: that these arguments have never been intrinsically even plausible, but have seemed so because they were secretly weighted by our wishes. Now I do not doubt that this sort of thing happens in thinking about religion as in thinking about other things: but as a general explanation of religious assent it seems to me quite useless. On that issue our wishes may favour either side or both. The assumption that every man would be pleased, and nothing but pleased, if only he could conclude that Christianity is true, appears to me to be simply preposterous. If Freud is right about the Oedipus complex, the universal pressure of the wish that God should not exist must be enormous, and atheism must be an admirable gratification to one of our strongest suppressed impulses. This argument, in fact, could be used on the theistic side. But I have no intention of so using it. It will not really help either party. It is fatally ambivalent. Men wish on both sides: and again, there is fear-fulfilment as well as wish-fulfilment, and hypochondriac temperaments will always tend to think true what they most wish to be false. Thus instead of the one predicament on which our opponents sometimes concentrate there are in fact four. A man may be a

Christian because he wants Christianity to be true. He may be an atheist because he wants atheism to be true. He may be an atheist because he wants Christianity to be true. He may be a Christian because he wants atheism to be true. Surely these possibilities cancel one another out? They may be of some use in analysing a particular instance of belief or disbelief, where we know the case history, but as a general explanation of either they will not help us. I do not think they overthrow the view that there is evidence both for and against the Christian propositions which fully rational minds, working honestly, can assess differently.

I therefore ask you to substitute a different and less tidy picture for that with which we began. In it, you remember, two different kinds of men, scientists, who proportioned their belief to the evidence, and Christians, who did not, were left facing one another across a chasm. The picture I should prefer is like this. All men alike, on questions which interest them, escape from the region of belief into that of knowledge when they can, and if they succeed in knowing, they no longer say they believe. The questions in which mathematicians are interested admit of treatment by a particularly clear and strict technique. Those of the scientist have their own technique, which is not quite the same. Those of the historian and the judge are different again. The mathematician's proof (at least so we laymen suppose) is by reasoning, the scientist's by experiment, the historian's by documents, the judge's by concurring sworn testimony. But all these men, as men, on questions outside their own disciplines, have numerous beliefs to which they do not normally apply the methods of their own disciplines. It would indeed carry some suspicion of morbidity and even of insanity if they did. These beliefs vary in strength from weak opinon to complete subjective certitude. Specimens of such beliefs at the strongest are the Christian's "I believe" and the convinced atheist's "I don't believe a word of it". The particular subject-matter on which these two disagree does not, of course, necessarily involve such strength of belief and disbelief. There are some who moderately opine that there is, or is not, a God. But there are others whose belief or disbelief is free from doubt. And all these beliefs, weak or strong, are based on what appears to the holders to be evidence; but the strong believers or disbelievers of course think they have very strong evidence. There is no need to suppose stark unreason on either side. We need only suppose error. One side has estimated the evidence wrongly. And even so, the mistake cannot be supposed to be of a flagrant nature; otherwise the debate would not continue.

So much, then, for the way in which Christians come to assent to certain propositions. But we have now to consider something quite different; their adherence to their belief after it has once been formed. It is here that the charge of irrationality and resistance to evidence becomes really important. For it must be admitted at once that Christians do praise such an adherence as if it were meritorious; and even, in a sense, more meritorious the stronger the apparent evidence against their faith becomes. They even warn one another that such apparent contrary evidence—such "trials to faith" or "temptations to doubt"—may be expected to occur, and determine in advance to resist them. And this is certainly shockingly unlike the behaviour we all demand of the scientist or the historian in their own disciplines. There, to slur over or ignore the faintest evidence against a favourite hypothesis, is admittedly foolish and shameful. It must be exposed to every test; every doubt must be invited. But then I do not admit that a hypothesis is a belief. And if we consider the scientist not among his hypotheses in the laboratory but among the beliefs in his ordinary life, I think the contrast between him and the Christian would be weakened. If, for the first time, a doubt of his wife's fidelity crosses the scientist's mind, does he consider it his duty at once to entertain this doubt with complete impartiality, at once to evolve a series of experiments by which it can be tested, and to await the result with pure neutrality of mind? No doubt it may come to that in the end. There are unfaithful wives; there are experimental husbands. But is such a course what his brother scientists would recommend to him (all of them, I suppose, except one) as the first step he should take and the only one consistent with his honour as a scientist? Or would they, like us, blame him for a moral flaw rather than praise him for an intellectual virtue if he did so?

This is intended, however, merely as a precaution against exaggerating the difference between Christian obstinacy in belief and the behaviour of normal people about their non-theological beliefs. I am far from suggesting that the case I have supposed is exactly parallel to the Christian obstinacy. For of course evidence of the wife's infidelity might accumulate, and presently reach a point at which the scientist would be pitiably foolish to disbelieve it. But the Christians seem to praise an adherence to the original belief which holds out against any evidence whatever. I must now try to show why such praise is in fact a logical conclusion from the original belief itself.

This can be done best by thinking for a moment of situations in which the thing is reversed. In Christianity such faith is demanded of us; but there are situations in which we demand it of others. There are times when we can do all that a fellow creature needs if only he will trust us. In getting a dog out of a trap, in extracting a thorn from a child's finger, in teaching a boy to swim or rescuing one who can't, in getting a frightened beginner over a nasty place on a mountain, the one fatal obstacle may be their distrust. We are asking them to trust us in the teeth of their senses, their imagination, and their intelligence. We ask them to believe that what is painful will relieve their pain and that what looks dangerous is their only safety. We ask them to accept apparent impossibilities : that moving the paw farther back into the trap is the way to get it out—that hurting the finger very much more will stop the finger hurting—that water which is obviously permeable will resist and support the body—that holding on to the only support within reach is not the way to avoid sinking—that to go higher and on to a more exposed ledge is the way not to fall. To support all these *incredibilia* we can rely only on the other party's confidence in us—a confidence certainly not based on demonstration, admittedly shot through with emotion, and perhaps, if we are strangers, resting on nothing but such assurance as the look of our face and the tone of our voice can supply, or even, for the dog, on our smell. Sometimes, because of their unbelief, we can do no mighty works. But if we succeed, we do so because they have maintained their faith in us against apparently contrary evidence. No one blames us for demanding such faith. No one blames them for giving it. No one says afterwards what an unintelligent dog or child or boy

that must have been to trust us. If the young mountain-
eer were a scientist, it would not be held against him,
when he came up for a fellowship, that he had once de-
parted from Clifford's rule of evidence by entertaining a
belief with strength greater than the evidence logically
obliged him to.

Now to accept the Christian propositions is *ipso facto*
to believe that we are to God, always, as that dog or child
or bather or mountain climber was to us, only very much
more so. From this it is a strictly logical conclusion that
the behaviour which was appropriate to them will be
appropriate to us, only very much more so. Mark: I am
not saying that the strength of our original belief must by
psychological necessity produce such behaviour. I am
saying that the content of our original belief by logical
necessity entails the proposition that such behaviour is
appropriate. If human life is in fact ordered by a beneficent being whose knowledge of our real needs and of the
way in which they can be satisfied infinitely exceeds our
own, we must expect *a priori* that His operations will
often appear to us far from beneficent and far from wise,
and that it will be our highest prudence to give Him our
confidence in spite of this. This expectation is increased
by the fact that when we accept Christianity we are
warned that apparent evidence against it will occur—
evidence strong enough " to deceive if possible the very
elect ". Our situation is rendered tolerable by two facts.
One is that we seem to ourselves, besides the apparently
contrary evidence, to receive favourable evidence. Some
of it is in the form of external events: as when I go to
see a man, moved by what I felt to be a whim, and find
he has been praying that I should come to him that day.
Some of it is more like the evidence on which the moun-

taineer or the dog might trust his rescuer—the rescuer's voice, look, and smell. For it seems to us (though you, on your premises, must believe us deluded) that we have something like a knowledge-by-acquaintance of the Person we believe in, however imperfect and intermittent it may be. We trust not because "a God" exists, but because *this* God exists. Or if we ourselves dare not claim to "know" Him, Christendom does, and we trust at least some of its representatives in the same way : because of the sort of people they are. The second fact is this. We think we can see already why, if our original belief is true, such trust beyond the evidence, against much apparent evidence, has to be demanded of us. For the question is not about being helped out of one trap or over one difficult place in a climb. We believe that His intention is to create a certain personal relation between Himself and us, a relation really *sui generis* but analogically describable in terms of filial or of erotic love. Complete trust is an ingredient in that relation—such trust as could have no room to grow except where there is also room for doubt. To love involves trusting the beloved beyond the evidence, even against much evidence. No man is our friend who believes in our good intentions only when they are proved. No man is our friend who will not be very slow to accept evidence against them. Such confidence, between one man and another, is in fact almost universally praised as a moral beauty, not blamed as a logical error. And the suspicious man is blamed for a meanness of character, not admired for the excellence of his logic.

There is, you see, no real parallel between Christian obstinacy in faith and the obstinacy of a bad scientist trying to preserve a hypothesis although the evidence has turned against it. Unbelievers very pardonably get the impression that an adherence to our faith is like that, because they meet Christianity, if at all, mainly in apologetic works. And there, of course, the existence and beneficence of God must appear as a speculative question like any other. Indeed, it is a speculative question as long as it is a question at all. But once it has been answered in the affirmative, you get quite a new situation. To believe that God—at least *this* God—exists is to believe that you as a person now stand in the presence of God as a Person. What would, a moment before, have been variations in opinion, now becomes variations in your personal attitude to a Person. You are no longer faced with an argument which demands your assent, but with a Person who demands your confidence. A faint analogy would be this. It is one thing to discuss *in vacuo* whether So-and-so will join us to-night, and another to discuss this when So-and-so's honour is pledged to come and some great matter depends on his coming. In the first case it would be merely reasonable, as the clock ticked on, to expect him less and less. In the second, a continued expectation far into the night would be due to our friend's character if we had found him reliable before. Which of us would not feel slightly ashamed if one moment after we had given him up he arrived with a full explanation of his delay? We should feel that we ought to have known him better.

Now of course we see, quite as clearly as you, how agonisingly two-edged all this is. A faith of this sort, if it happens to be true, is obviously what we need, and it is infinitely ruinous to lack it. But there can be faith of this sort where it is wholly ungrounded. The dog may lick the face of the man who comes to take it out of the trap; but the man may only mean to vivisect it in South Parks Road when he has done so. The ducks who come to the call "Dilly, dilly, come and be killed" have confidence in the farmer's wife, and she wrings their necks for their pains. There is that famous French story of the fire in the theatre. Panic was spreading, the spectators were just turning from an audience into a mob. At that moment a huge bearded man leaped through the orchestra on to the stage, raised his hand with a gesture full of nobility, and cried, "*Que chacun regagne sa place.*" Such was the authority of his voice and bearing that everyone obeyed him. As a result they were all burned to death, while the bearded man walked quietly out through the wings to the stage door, took a cab which was waiting for someone else, and went home to bed.

That demand for our confidence which a true friend makes of us is exactly the same that a confidence trickster would make. That refusal to trust, which is sensible in reply to a confidence trickster, is ungenerous and ignoble to a friend, and deeply damaging to our relation with him. To be forewarned and therefore forearmed against apparently contrary appearance is eminently rational if our belief is true; but if our belief is a delusion, this same forewarning and forearming would obviously be the method whereby the delusion rendered itself incurable. And yet again, to be aware of these possibilities and still to reject them is clearly the precise mode, and the only mode, in which our personal response to God can establish itself. In that sense the ambiguity is not something that conflicts with faith so much as a condition which makes faith possible. When you are asked for trust you may give it or withhold it; it is senseless to say that you will trust if you are given demonstrative certainty. There would be no room for trust if demonstration were given. When demonstration is given what will be left will be simply the sort of relation which results from having trusted, or not having trusted, before it was given.

The saying " Blessed are those that have not seen and have believed " has nothing to do with our original assent to the Christian propositions. It was not addressed to a philosopher inquiring whether God exists. It was addressed to a man who already believed that, who already had long acquaintance with a particular Person, and evidence that that Person could do very odd things, and who then refused to believe one odd thing more, often predicted by that Person and vouched for by all his closest friends. It is a rebuke not to scepticism in the philosophic sense but to the psychological quality of being " suspicious ". It says in effect, " You should have known me better." There are cases between man and man where we should all, in our different way, bless those who have not seen and have believed. Our relation to those who trusted us only after we were proved innocent in court cannot be the same as our relation to those who trusted us all through.

Our opponents, then, have a perfect right to dispute with us about the grounds of our original assent. But they must not accuse us of sheer insanity if, after the assent has been given, our adherence to it is no longer proportioned to every fluctuation of the apparent evidence. They cannot of course be expected to know on what our assurance feeds, and how it revives and is always rising from its ashes. They cannot be expected to see how the *quality* of the object which we think we are beginning to know by acquaintance drives us to the view that if this were a delusion then we should have to say that the universe had produced no real thing of comparable value and that all explanations of the delusion seemed somehow less important than the thing explained. That is knowledge we cannot communicate. But they can see how the assent, of necessity, moves us from the logic of speculative thought into what might perhaps be called the logic of personal relations. What would, up till then, have been variations simply of opinion become variations of conduct by a person to a Person. *Credere Deum esse* turns into *Credere in Deum*. And *Deum* here is this God, the increasingly knowable Lord.

The Oxford Socratic Club, 1955

TRANSPOSITION

In the church to which I belong this day is set apart for commemorating the descent of the Holy Ghost upon the first Christians shortly after the Ascension. I want to consider one of the phenomena which accompanied, or followed, this descent; the phenomenon which our translation calls "speaking with tongues" and which the learned call *glossolalia*. You will not suppose that I think this the most important aspect of Pentecost, but I have two reasons for selecting it. In the first place it would be ridiculous for me to speak about the nature of the Holy Ghost or the modes of His operation: that would be an attempt to teach when I have nearly all to learn. In the second place, *glossolalia* has often been a stumbling-block to me. It is, to be frank, an embarrassing phenomenon. St. Paul himself seems to have been rather embarrassed by it in I Corinthians and labours to turn the desire and the attention of the Church to more obviously edifying gifts. But he goes no further. He throws in almost parenthetically the statement that he himself spoke with tongues more than anyone else, and he does not question the spiritual, or supernatural, source of the phenomenon.

The difficulty I feel is this. On the one hand, *glossolalia* has remained an intermittent "variety of religious experience" down to the present day. Every now and then we hear that in some revivalist meeting one or more of those present has burst into a torrent of what appears to be gibberish. The thing does not seem to be edifying,

75

and all non-Christian opinion would regard it as a kind of hysteria, an involuntary discharge of nervous excitement. A good deal even of Christian opinion would explain most instances of it in exactly the same way; and I must confess that it would be very hard to believe that in all instances of it the Holy Ghost is operating. We suspect, even if we cannot be sure, that it is usually an affair of the nerves. That is one horn of the dilemma. On the other hand, we cannot as Christians shelve the story of Pentecost or deny that there, at any rate, the speaking with tongues was miraculous. For the men spoke not gibberish but languages unknown to them though known to other people present. And the whole event of which this makes part is built into the very fabric of the birth-story of the Church. It is this very event which the risen Lord has told the Church to wait for—almost in the last words He uttered before His ascension. It looks, therefore, as if we shall have to say that the very same phenomenon which is sometimes not only natural but even pathological is at other times (or at least at one other time) the organ of the Holy Ghost. And this seems at first very surprising and very open to attack. The sceptic will certainly seize this opportunity to talk to us about Occam's razor, to accuse us of multiplying hypotheses. If most instances of *glossolalia* are covered by hysteria, is it not (he will ask) extremely probable that that explanation covers the remaining instances too?

It is to this difficulty that I would gladly bring a little ease if I can. And I will begin by pointing out that it belongs to a class of difficulties. The closest parallel to it within that class is raised by the erotic language and imagery we find in the mystics. In them we find a whole range of expressions—and therefore possibly of emotions

—with which we are quite familiar in another context and which, in that other context, have a clear natural significance. But in the mystical writings it is claimed that these elements have a different cause. And once more the sceptic will ask why the cause which we are content to accept for ninety-nine instances of such language should not be held to cover the hundredth too. The hypothesis that mysticism is an erotic phenomenon will seem to him immensely more probable than any other.

Put in its most general terms our problem is that of the obvious continuity between things which are admittedly natural and things which, it is claimed, are spiritual; the reappearance in what professes to be our supernatural life of all the same old elements which make up our natural life and (it would seem) of no others. If we have really been visited by a revelation from beyond Nature, is it not very strange that an Apocalypse can furnish heaven with nothing more than selections from terrestrial experience (crowns, thrones, and music), that devotion can find no language but that of human lovers, and that the rite whereby Christians enact a mystical union should turn out to be only the old, familiar act of eating and drinking? And you may add that the very same problem also breaks out on a lower level, not only between spiritual and natural but also between higher and lower levels of the natural life. Hence cynics very plausibly challenge our civilised conception of the difference between love and lust by pointing out that when all is said and done they usually end in what is, physically, the same act. They similarly challenge the difference between justice and revenge on the ground that what finally happens to the criminal may be the same. And in all these cases, let us admit that the cynics and sceptics have a good *prima facie* case. The same acts do reappear in justice as well as in revenge : the consummation of humanised and conjugal love is physiologically the same as that of the merely biological lust; religious language and imagery, and probably religious emotion too, contains nothing that has not been borrowed from Nature.

Now it seems to me that the only way to refute the critic here is to show that the same *prima facie* case is equally plausible in some instance where we all know (not by faith or by logic, but empirically) that it is in fact false. Can we find an instance of higher and lower where the higher is within almost everyone's experience? I think we can. Consider the following quotation from *Pepys's Diary* :

> With my wife to the King's House to see *The Virgin Martyr*, and it is mighty pleasant. . . . But that which did please me beyond anything in the whole world was the wind musick when the angel comes down, which is so sweet that it ravished me and, indeed, in a word, did wrap up my soul so that it made me really sick, just as I have formerly been when in love with my wife . . . and makes me resolve to practise wind musick and to make my wife do the like. (27th February, 1688.)

There are several points here that deserve attention. Firstly that the internal sensation accompanying intense æsthetic delight was indistinguishable from the sensation accompanying two other experiences, that of being in love and that of being, say, in a rough channel crossing. (2) That of these two other experiences one at least is the very reverse of pleasurable. No man enjoys nausea.

(3) That Pepys was, nevertheless, anxious to have again the experience whose sensational accompaniment was identical with the very unpleasant accompaniments of sickness. That was why he decided to take up wind music.

Now it may be true that not many of us have fully shared Pepys's experience; but we have all experienced that sort of thing. For myself I find that if, during a moment of intense æsthetic rapture, one tries to turn round and catch by introspection what one is actually feeling, one can never lay one's hand on anything but a physical sensation. In my case it is a kind of kick or flutter in the diaphragm. Perhaps that is all Pepys meant by " really sick ". But the important point is this : I find that this kick or flutter is exactly the same sensation which, in me, accompanies great and sudden anguish. Introspection can discover no difference at all between my neural response to very bad news and my neural response to the overture of *The Magic Flute*. If I were to judge simply by sensations I should come to the absurd conclusion that joy and anguish are the same thing, that what I most dread is the same with what I most desire. Introspection discovers nothing more or different in the one than in the other. And I expect that most of you, if you are in the habit of noticing such things, will report more or less the same.

Now let us take a step farther. These sensations— Pepys's sickness and my flutter in the diaphragm—do not merely accompany very different experiences as an irrelevant or neutral addition. We may be quite sure that Pepys hated that sensation when it came in real sickness : and we know from his own words that he liked it when it came with wind music, for he took measures to make as sure as possible of getting it again. And I likewise love this internal flutter in one context and call it a pleasure and hate it in another and call it misery. It is not a mere sign of joy and anguish : it becomes what it signifies. When the joy thus flows over into the nerves, that overflow is its consummation : when the anguish thus flows over, that physical symptom is the crowning horror. The very same thing which makes the sweetest drop of all in the sweet cup also makes the bitterest drop in the bitter.

And here, I suggest, we have found what we are looking for. I take our emotional life to be " higher " than the life of our sensations—not, of course, morally higher, but richer, more varied, more subtle. And this is a higher level which nearly all of us know. And I believe that if anyone watches carefully the relation between his emotions and his sensations he will discover the following facts : (1) that the nerves do respond, and in a sense most adequately and exquisitely, to the emotions; (2) that their resources are far more limited, the possible variations of sense far fewer, than those of emotion; (3) and that the senses compensate for this by using the *same* sensation to express more than one emotion—even, as we have seen, to express opposite emotions.

Where we tend to go wrong is in assuming that if there is to be a correspondence between two systems it must be a one for one correspondence—that A in the one system must be represented by *a* in the other, and so on. But the correspondence between emotion and sensation turns out not to be of that sort. And there never could be correspondence of that sort where the one system was really richer than the other. If the richer system is to be represented in the poorer at all, this can only be by giving each element in the poorer system more than one meaning. The transposition of the richer into the poorer must, so to speak, be algebraical, not arithmetical. If you are to translate from a language which has a large vocabulary into a language that has a small vocabulary, then you must be allowed to use several words in more than one sense. If you are to write a language with twenty-two vowel sounds in an alphabet with only five vowel characters then you must be allowed to give each of those five characters more than one value. If you are making a piano version of a piece originally scored for an orchestra, then the same piano notes which represent flutes in one passage must also represent violins in another.

As the examples show we are all quite familiar with this kind of transposition or adaptation from a richer to a poorer medium. The most familiar example of all is the art of drawing. The problem here is to represent a three-dimensional world on a flat sheet of paper. The solution is perspective, and perspective means that we must give more than one value to a two-dimensional shape. Thus in a drawing of a cube we use an acute angle to represent what is a right angle in the real world. But elsewhere an acute angle on the paper may represent what was already an acute angle in the real world : for example, the point of a spear or the gable of a house. The very same shape which you must draw to give the illusion of a straight road receding from the spectator is also the shape you draw for a dunce's cap. As with the lines, so with the shading. Your brightest light in the picture is, in literal fact, only plain white paper : and this must do for the sun, or a lake in evening light, or snow, or human flesh.

I now make two comments on the instances of Transposition which are already before us:

(1) It is clear that in each case what is happening in the lower medium can be understood only if we know the higher medium. The instance where this knowledge is most commonly lacking is the musical one. The piano version means one thing to the musician who knows the original orchestral score and another thing to the man who hears it simply as a piano piece. But the second man would be at an even greater disadvantage if he had never heard any instrument but a piano and even doubted the existence of other instruments. Even more, we understand pictures only because we know and inhabit the three-dimensional world. If we can imagine a creature who perceived only two dimensions and yet could somehow be aware of the lines as he crawled over them on the paper, we shall easily see how impossible it would be for him to understand. At first he might be prepared to accept on authority our assurance that there was a world in three dimensions. But when we pointed to the lines on the paper and tried to explain, say, that "This is a road", would be not reply that the shape which we were asking him to accept as a revelation of our mysterious other world was the very same shape which, on our own showing, elsewhere meant nothing but a triangle. And soon, I think, he would say, "You keep on telling me of this other world and its unimaginable shapes which you call solid. But isn't it very suspicious that all the shapes which you offer me as images or reflections of the solid ones turn out on inspection to be simply the old two-dimensional shapes of my own world as I have always known it? Is it not obvious that your vaunted other world, so far from being the archetype, is

a dream which borrows all its elements from this one?"

(2) It is of some importance to notice that the word *symbolism* is not adequate in all cases to cover the relation between the higher medium and its transposition in the lower. It covers some cases perfectly, but not others. Thus the relation between speech and writing is one of symbolism. The written characters exist solely for the eye, the spoken words solely for the ear. There is complete discontinuity between them. They are not like one another, nor does the one cause the other to be. The one is simply a *sign* of the other and signifies it by a convention. But a picture is not related to the visible world in just that way. Pictures are part of the visible world themselves and represent it only by being part of it. Their visibility has the same source. The suns and lamps in pictures seem to shine only because real suns or lamps shine on them: that is, they seem to shine a great deal because they really shine a little in reflecting their archetypes. The sunlight in a picture is therefore not related to real sunlight simply as written words are to spoken. It is a sign, but also something more than a sign: and only a sign because it is also more than a sign, because in it the thing signified is really in a certain mode present. If I had to name the relation I should call it not symbolical but sacramental. But in the case we started from—that of emotion and sensation—we are even further beyond mere symbolism. For there, as we have seen, the very same sensation does not merely accompany, nor merely signify, diverse and opposite emotions, but becomes part of them. The emotion descends bodily, as it were, into the sensation and digests, transforms, transubstantiates it, so that the same thrill along the nerves *is* delight or *is* agony.

I am not going to maintain that what I call Transposition is the only possible mode whereby a poorer medium can respond to a richer : but I claim that it is very hard to imagine any other. It is therefore, at the very least, not improbable that Transposition occurs whenever the higher reproduces itself in the lower. Thus, to digress for a moment, it seems to me very likely that the real relation between mind and body is one of Transposition. We are certain that, in this life at any rate, thought is intimately connected with the brain. The theory that thought therefore is merely a movement in the brain is, in my opinion, nonsense; for if so, that theory itself would be merely a movement, an event among atoms, which may have speed and direction but of which it would be meaningless to use the words " true " or " false ". We are driven then to some kind of correspondence. But if we assume a one-for-one correspondence this means that we have to attribute an almost unbelievable complexity and variety of events to the brain. But I submit that a one-for-one relation is probably quite unnecessary. All our examples suggest that the brain can respond—in a sense, adequately and exquisitely correspond—to the seemingly infinite variety of consciousness without providing one single physical modification for each single modification of consciousness.

But that is a digression. Let us now return to our original question, about Spirit and Nature, God and Man. Our problem was that in what claims to be our spiritual life all the elements of our natural life recur : and, what is worse, it looks at first glance as if no other elements were present. We now see that if the spiritual is richer than the natural (as no one who believes in its existence would deny) then this is exactly what we should expect. And the sceptic's conclusion that the so-called spiritual is really derived from the natural, that it is a mirage or projection or imaginary extension of the natural, is also exactly what we should expect; for, as we have seen, this is the mistake which an observer who knew only the lower medium would be bound to make in every case of Transposition. The brutal man never can by analysis find anything but lust in love; the Flatlander never can find anything but flat shapes in a picture; physiology never can find anything in thought except twitchings of the grey matter. It is no good browbeating the critic who approaches a Transposition from below. On the evidence available to him his conclusion is the only one possible.

Everything is different when you approach the Transposition from above, as we all do in the case of emotion and sensation or of the three-dimensional world and pictures, and as the spiritual man does in the case we are considering. Those who spoke with tongues, as St. Paul did, can well understand how that holy phenomenon differed from the hysterical phenomenon—although be it remembered, they were in a sense exactly the same phenomenon, just as the very same sensation came to Pepys in love, in the enjoyment of music, and in sickness. Spiritual things are spiritually discerned. The spiritual man judges all things and is judged of none.

But who dares claim to be a spiritual man? In the full sense, none of us. And yet we are somehow aware that we approach from above, or from inside, at least some of those Transpositions which embody the Christian life in this world. With whatever sense of unworthiness, with whatever sense of audacity, we must affirm that we know a little of the higher system which is being transposed. In a way the claim we are making is not a very startling one. We are only claiming to know that our apparent devotion, whatever else it may have been, was not simply erotic, or that our apparent desire for Heaven, whatever else it may have been, was not simply a desire for longevity or jewellery or social splendours. Perhaps we have never really attained at all to what St. Paul would describe as spiritual life. But at the very least we know, in some dim and confused way, that we were trying to use natural acts and images and language with a new value, have at least desired a repentance which was not merely prudential and a love which was not self-centred. At the worst, we know enough of the spiritual to know that we have fallen short of it : as if the picture knew enough of the three-dimensional world to be aware that it was flat.

It is not only for humility's sake (that, of course) that we must emphasise the dimness of our knowledge. I suspect that, save by God's direct miracle, spiritual experience can never abide introspection. If even our emotions will not do so (since the attempt to find out what we are now *feeling* yields nothing more than a physical sensation), much less will the operations of the Holy Ghost. The attempt to discover by introspective analysis our own spiritual condition is to me a horrible thing which reveals, at best, not the secrets of God's spirit and ours, but their transpositions in intellect, emotion and imagination, and which at worst may be the quickest road to presumption or despair.

I believe that this doctrine of Transposition provides for most of us a background very much needed for the theological virtue of Hope. We can hope only for what we can desire. And the trouble is that any adult and philosophically respectable notion we can form of Heaven is forced to deny of that state most of the things our nature desires. There is no doubt a blessedly ingenuous faith, a child's or a savage's faith which finds no difficulty. It accepts without awkward questionings the harps and golden streets and the family reunions pictured by hymn-writers. Such a faith is deceived, yet, in the deepest sense, not deceived; for while it errs in mistaking symbol for fact, yet it apprehends Heaven as joy and plenitude and love. But it is impossible for most of us. And we must not try, by artifice, to make ourselves more naïf than we are. A man does not "become as a little child " by aping childhood. Hence our notion of Heaven involves perpetual negations; no food, no drink, no sex, no movement, no mirth, no events, no time, no art.

Against all these, to be sure, we set one positive : the vision and enjoyment of God. And since this is an infinite good we hold (rightly) that it outweighs them all. That is, the reality of the Beatific Vision would, or will, outweigh, would infinitely outweigh, the reality of the negations. But can our present notion of it outweigh our present notion of them? That is quite a different question. And for most of us at most times the answer is No. How it may be for great saints and mystics I cannot tell. But for others the conception of that Vision is a difficult, precarious and fugitive extrapolation from a very few and ambiguous moments in our earthly experience : while our idea of the negated natural goods is vivid and persistent, loaded with the memories of a lifetime, built into our nerves and muscles and therefore into our imaginations.

Thus the negatives have, so to speak, an unfair advantage in every competition with the positive. What is worse, their presence—and most when we most resolutely

try to suppress or ignore them—vitiates even such a faint
and ghostlike notion of the positive as we might have
had. The exclusion of the lower goods begins to seem the
essential characteristic of the higher good. We feel, if we
do not say, that the vision of God will come not to fulfil
but to destroy our nature; this bleak fantasy often under-
lies our very use of such words as " holy " or " pure " or
" spiritual ".

We must not allow this to happen if we can possibly
prevent it. We must believe—and therefore in some degree imagine—that every negation will be only the
reverse side of a fulfilling. And we must mean by that
the fulfilling, precisely, of our humanity; not our trans-
formation into angels nor our absorption into Deity. For
though we shall be " as the angels " and made " like
unto " our Master, I think this means " like with the like-
ness proper to men " : as different instruments that play
the same air but each in its own fashion. How far the
life of the risen man will be sensory, we do not know. But
I surmise that it will differ from the sensory life we know
here, not as emptiness differs from water or water from
wine but as a flower differs from a bulb or a cathedral
from an architect's drawing. And it is here that Transposition helps me.

Let us construct a fable. Let us picture a woman
thrown into a dungeon. There she bears and rears a son.
He grows up seeing nothing but the dungeon walls, the
straw on the floor, and a little patch of the sky seen
through the grating, which is too high up to show anything except sky. This unfortunate woman was an artist,
and when they imprisoned her she managed to bring
with her a drawing pad and a box of pencils. As she
never loses the hope of deliverance she is constantly

teaching her son about that outer world which he has never seen. She does it very largely by drawing him pictures. With her pencil she attempts to show him what fields, rivers, mountains, cities and waves on a beach are like. He is a dutiful boy and he does his best to believe her when she tells him that that outer world is far more interesting and glorious than anything in the dungeon. At times he succeeds. On the whole he gets on tolerably well until, one day, he says something that gives his mother pause. For a minute or two they are at cross-purposes. Finally it dawns on her that he has, all these years, lived under a misconception. " But ", she gasps, "you didn't think that the real world was full of lines drawn in lead pencil?" " What?" says the boy. " No pencil-marks there?" And instantly his whole notion of the outer world becomes a blank. For the lines, by which alone he was imagining it, have now been denied of it. He has no idea of that which will exclude and dispense with the lines, that of which the lines were merely a transposition—the waving tree-tops, the light dancing on the weir, the coloured three-dimensional realities which are not enclosed in lines but define their own shapes at every moment with a delicacy and multiplicity which no drawing could ever achieve. The child will get the idea that the real world is somehow less visible than his mother's pictures. In reality it lacks lines because it is incomparably more visible.

So with us. " We know not what we shall be "; but we may be sure we shall be more, not less, than we were on earth. Our natural experiences (sensory, emotional, imaginative) are only like the drawing, like pencilled lines on flat paper. If they vanish in the risen life, they will vanish only as pencil lines vanish from the real landscape; not as a candle flame that is put out but as a candle flame which becomes invisible because someone has pulled up the blind, thrown open the shutters, and let in the blaze of the risen sun.

You can put it whichever way you please. You can say that by Transposition our humanity, senses and all, can be made the vehicle of beatitude. Or you can say that the heavenly bounties by Transposition are embodied during this life in our temporal experience. But the second way is the better. It is the present life which is the diminution, the symbol, the etiolated, the (as it were) " vegetarian " substitute. If flesh and blood cannot inherit the Kingdom, that is not because they are too solid, too gross, too distinct, too " illustrious with being ". They are too flimsy, too transitory, too phantasmal.

With this my case, as the lawyers say, is complete. But I have just four points to add :

1. I hope it is quite clear that the conception of Transposition, as I call it, is distinct from another conception often used for the same purpose—I mean the conception of development. The Developmentalist explains the continuity between things that claim to be spiritual and things that are certainly natural by saying that the one slowly turned into the other. I believe this view explains some facts, but I think it has been much overworked. At any rate it is not the theory I am putting forward. I am not saying that the natural act of eating after millions of years somehow blossoms into the Christian sacrament. I am saying that the Spiritual Reality, which existed before there were any creatures who ate, gives this natural act a new meaning, and more than a new meaning : makes it in a certain context to be a different thing. In a word, I think that real landscapes enter into pictures, not that

pictures will one day sprout out into real trees and grass.

2. I have found it impossible, in thinking of what I call Transposition, not to ask myself whether it may help us to conceive the Incarnation. Of course if Transposition were merely a mode of symbolism it could give us no help at all in this matter : on the contrary, it would lead us wholly astray, back into a new kind of Docetism (or would it be only the old kind?) and away from the utterly historical and concrete reality which is the centre of all our hope, faith and love. But then, as I have pointed out, Transposition is not always symbolism. In varying degrees the lower reality can actually be drawn into the higher and become part of it. The sensation which accompanies joy becomes itself joy : we can hardly choose but say "incarnates joy". If this is so, then I venture to suggest, though with great doubt and in the most provisional way, that the concept of Transposition may have some contribution to make to the theology—or at least to the philosophy—of the Incarnation. For we are told in one of the creeds that the Incarnation worked "not by conversion of the Godhead into flesh, but by taking of the Manhood into God". And it seems to me that there is a real analogy between this and what I have called Transposition : that humanity, still remaining itself, is not merely counted as, but veritably drawn into, Deity, seems to me like what happens when a sensation (not in itself a pleasure) is drawn into the joy it accompanies. But I walk *in mirabilibus supra me* and submit all to the verdict of real theologians.

3. I have tried to stress throughout the inevitableness of the error made about every transposition by one who approaches it from the lower medium only. The strength of such a critic lies in the words "merely" or "nothing

but ". He sees all the facts but not the meaning. Quite truly, therefore, he claims to have seen all the facts. There *is* nothing else there; except the meaning. He is therefore, as regards the matter in hand, in the position of an animal. You will have noticed that most dogs cannot understand *pointing*. You point to a bit of food on the floor : the dog, instead of looking at the floor, sniffs at your finger. A finger is a finger to him, and that is all. His world is all fact and no meaning. And in a period when factual realism is dominant we shall find people deliberately inducing upon themselves this dog-like mind. A man who has experienced love from within will deliberately go about to inspect it analytically from outside and regard the results of this analysis as truer than his experience. The extreme limit of this self-blinding is seen in those who, like the rest of us, have consciousness, yet go about to study the human organism as if they did not know it was conscious. As long as this deliberate refusal to understand things from above, even where such understanding is possible, continues, it is idle to talk of any final victory over materialism. The critique of every experience from below, the voluntary ignoring of meaning and concentration on fact, will always have the same plausibility. There will always be evidence, and every month fresh evidence, to show that religion is only psychological, justice only self-protection, politics only economics, love only lust, and thought itself only cerebral biochemistry.

4. Finally, I suggest that what has been said of Transposition throws a new light on the doctrine of the resurrection of the body. For in a sense Transposition can do anything. However great the difference between Spirit and Nature, between æsthetic joy and that flutter in the

diaphragm, between reality and picture, yet the Transposition can be in its own way adequate. I said before that in your drawing you had only plain white paper for sun and cloud, snow, water, and human flesh. In one sense, how miserably inadequate! Yet in another, how perfect. If the shadows are properly done, that patch of white paper will, in some curious way, be very like blazing sunshine; we shall almost feel cold while we look at the paper snow and almost warm our hands at the paper fire. May we not, by a reasonable analogy, suppose likewise that there is no experience of the spirit so transcendent and supernatural, no vision of Deity Himself so close and so far beyond all images and emotions, that to it there cannot be an appropriate correspondence on the sensory level? Not by a new sense but by the incredible flooding of those very sensations we now have with a meaning, a transvaluation, of which we have here no faintest guess?

A Sermon at Mansfield College, Oxford

THE WEIGHT OF GLORY

If you asked twenty good men to-day what they thought the highest of the virtues, nineteen of them would reply, Unselfishness. But if you had asked almost any of the great Christians of old he would have replied, Love. You see what has happened? A negative term has been substituted for a positive, and this is of more than philological importance. The negative idea of Unselfishness carries with it the suggestion not primarily of securing good things for others, but of going without them ourselves, as if our abstinence and not their happiness was the important point. I do not think this is the Christian virtue of Love. The New Testament has lots to say about self-denial, but not about self-denial as an end in itself. We are told to deny ourselves and to take up our crosses in order that we may follow Christ; and nearly every description of what we shall ultimately find if we do so contains an appeal to desire. If there lurks in most modern minds the notion that to desire our own good and earnestly to hope for the enjoyment of it is a bad thing, I submit that this notion has crept in from Kant and the Stoics and is no part of the Christian faith. Indeed, if we consider the unblushing promises of reward and the staggering nature of the rewards promised in the Gospels, it would seem that Our Lord finds our desires, not too strong, but too weak. We are half-hearted creatures, fooling about with drink and sex and ambition when infinite joy is offered us, like an ignorant child who wants to go on making mud pies in a slum because he cannot imagine what is meant by the offer of a holiday at the sea. We are far too easily pleased.

We must not be troubled by unbelievers when they say that this promise of reward makes the Christian life a mercenary affair. There are different kinds of reward. There is the reward which has no natural connection with the things you do to earn it, and is quite foreign to the desires that ought to accompany those things. Money is not the natural reward of love, that is why we call a man mercenary if he marries a woman for the sake of her money. But marriage is the proper reward for a real lover, and he is not mercenary for desiring it. A general who fights well in order to get a peerage is mercenary; a general who fights for victory is not, victory being the proper reward of battle as marriage is the proper reward of love. The proper rewards are not simply tacked on to the activity for which they are given, but are the activity itself in consummation. There is also a third case, which is more complicated. An enjoyment of Greek poetry is certainly a proper, and not a mercenary, reward for learning Greek; but only those who have reached the stage of enjoying Greek poetry can tell from their own experience that this is so. The schoolboy beginning Greek grammar cannot look forward to his adult enjoyment of Sophocles as a lover looks forward to marriage or a general to victory. He has to begin by working for marks, or to escape punishment, or to please his parents, or, at best, in the hope of a future good which he cannot at present imagine or desire. His position, therefore, bears a certain resemblance to that of the mercenary; the reward he is going to get will, in actual fact, be a natural or proper reward, but he will not know that till he has got it. Of course, he gets it gradually; enjoyment creeps in upon the mere drudgery, and nobody could point to a day or an hour when the one ceased and the other began. But it is just in so far as he approaches the reward that he becomes able to desire it for its own sake; indeed, the power of so desiring it is itself a preliminary reward.

The Christian, in relation to heaven, is in much the same position as this schoolboy. Those who have attained everlasting life in the vision of God doubtless know very well that it is no mere bribe, but the very consummation of their earthly discipleship; but we who have not yet attained it cannot know this in the same way, and cannot even begin to know it at all except by continuing to obey and finding the first reward of our obedience in our increasing power to desire the ultimate reward. Just in proportion as the desire grows, our fear lest it should be a mercenary desire will die away and finally be recognised as an absurdity. But probably this will not, for most of us, happen in a day; poetry replaces grammar, gospel replaces law, longing transforms obedience, as gradually as the tide lifts a grounded ship.

But there is one other important similarity between the schoolboy and ourselves. If he is an imaginative boy he will, quite probably, be revelling in the English poets and romancers suitable to his age some time before he begins to suspect that Greek grammar is going to lead him to more and more enjoyments of this same sort. He may even be neglecting his Greek to read Shelley and Swinburne in secret. In other words, the desire which Greek is really going to gratify already exists in him and is attached to objects which seem to him quite unconnected with Xenophon and the verbs in $\mu\iota$. Now, if we are made for heaven, the desire for our proper place will be already in us, but not yet attached to the true object, and will even appear as the rival of that object. And this, I think, is just what we find. No doubt there is one point in which my analogy of the schoolboy breaks down. The English poetry which he reads when he ought to be doing Greek exercises may be just as good as the Greek poetry to which the exercises are leading him, so that in fixing on Milton instead of journeying on to Aeschylus his desire is not embracing a false object. But our case is very different. If a transtemporal, transfinite good is our real destiny, then any other good on which our desire fixes must be in some degree fallacious, must bear at best only a symbolical relation to what will truly satisfy.

In speaking of this desire for our own far-off country, which we find in ourselves even now, I feel a certain shyness. I am almost committing an indecency. I am trying to rip open the inconsolable secret in each one of you—the secret which hurts so much that you take your revenge on it by calling it names like Nostalgia and Romanticism and Adolescence; the secret also which pierces with such sweetness that when, in very intimate conversation, the mention of it becomes imminent, we grow awkward and affect to laugh at ourselves; the secret we cannot hide and cannot tell, though we desire to do both. We cannot tell it because it is a desire for something that has never actually appeared in our experience. We cannot hide it because our experience is constantly suggesting it, and we betray ourselves like lovers at the mention of a name. Our commonest expedient is to call it beauty and behave as if that had settled the matter. Wordsworth's expedient was to identify it with certain moments in his own past. But all this is a cheat. If Wordsworth had gone back to those moments in the past,

he would not have found the thing itself, but only the
reminder of it; what he remembered would turn out to
be itself a remembering. The books or the music in
which we thought the beauty was located will betray us if
we trust to them; it was not *in* them, it only came
through them, and what came through them was longing. These things—the beauty, the memory of our own
past—are good images of what we really desire; but if
they are mistaken for the thing itself they turn into dumb
idols, breaking the hearts of their worshippers. For they
are not the thing itself; they are only the scent of a flower
we have not found, the echo of a tune we have not heard,
news from a country we have never yet visited. Do you
think I am trying to weave a spell? Perhaps I am; but
remember your fairy tales. Spells are used for breaking
enchantments as well as for inducing them. And you and
I have need of the strongest spell that can be found to
wake us from the evil enchantment of worldliness which
has been laid upon us for nearly a hundred years. Almost
our whole education has been directed to silencing this
shy, persistent, inner voice; almost all our modern philosophies have been devised to convince us that the good
of man is to be found on this earth. And yet it is a
remarkable thing that such philosophies of Progress or
Creative Evolution themselves bear reluctant witness to
the truth that our real goal is elsewhere. When they want
to convince you that earth is your home, notice how they
set about it. They begin by trying to persuade you that
earth can be made into heaven, thus giving a sop to your
sense of exile in earth as it is. Next, they tell you that this
fortunate event is still a good way off in the future, thus
giving a sop to your knowledge that the fatherland is not
here and now. Finally, lest your longing for the trans-

temporal should awake and spoil the whole affair, they use any rhetoric that comes to hand to keep out of your mind the recollection that even if all the happiness they promised could come to man on earth, yet still each generation would lose it by death, including the last generation of all, and the whole story would be nothing, not even a story, for ever and ever. Hence all the nonsense that Mr. Shaw puts into the final speech of Lilith, and Bergson's remark that the *élan vital* is capable of surmounting all obstacles, perhaps even death—as if we could believe that any social or biological development on this planet will delay the senility of the sun or reverse the second law of thermodynamics.

Do what they will, then, we remain conscious of a desire which no natural happiness will satisfy. But is there any reason to suppose that reality offers any satisfaction to it? " Nor does the being hungry prove that we have bread." But I think it may be urged that this misses the point. A man's physical hunger does not prove that that man will get any bread; he may die of starvation on a raft in the Atlantic. But surely a man's hunger does prove that he comes of a race which repairs its body by eating and inhabits a world where eatable substances exist. In the same way, though I do not believe (I wish I did) that my desire for Paradise proves that I shall enjoy it, I think it a pretty good indication that such a thing exists and that some men will. A man may love a woman and not win her; but it would be very odd if the phenomenon called " falling in love " occurred in a sexless world.

Here, then, is the desire, still wandering and uncertain of its object and still largely unable to see that object in the direction where it really lies. Our sacred books give us some account of the object. It is, of course, a symbolical account. Heaven is, by definition, outside our experience, but all intelligible descriptions must be of things within our experience. The scriptural picture of heaven is therefore just as symbolical as the picture which our desire, unaided, invents for itself; heaven is not really full of jewellery any more than it is really the beauty of Nature, or a fine piece of music. The difference is that the scriptural imagery has authority. It comes to us from writers who were closer to God than we, and it has stood the test of Christian experience down the centuries. The natural appeal of this authoritative imagery is to me, at first, very small. At first sight it chills, rather than awakes, my desire. And that is just what I ought to expect. If Christianity could tell me no more of the far-off land than my own temperament led me to surmise already, then Christianity would be no higher than myself. If it has more to give me, I must expect it to be less immediately attractive than " my own stuff ". Sophocles at first seems dull and cold to the boy who has only reached Shelley. If our religion is something objective, then we must never avert our eyes from those elements in it which seem puzzling or repellent; for it will be precisely the puzzling or the repellent which conceals what we do not yet know and need to know.

The promises of Scripture may very roughly be reduced to five heads. It is promised, firstly, that we shall be with Christ; secondly, that we shall be like Him; thirdly, with an enormous wealth of imagery, that we shall have " glory "; fourthly, that we shall, in some sense, be fed or feasted or entertained; and, finally, that we shall have some sort of official position in the universe—ruling cities, judging angels, being pillars of God's

temple. The first question I ask about these promises is:
" Why any of them except the first?" Can anything be
added to the conception of being with Christ? For it
must be true, as an old writer says, that he who has God
and everything else has no more than he who has God
only. I think the answer turns again on the nature
of symbols. For though it may escape our notice at first
glance, yet it is true that any conception of being with
Christ which most of us can now form will be not very
much less symbolical than the other promises; for it will
smuggle in ideas of proximity in space and loving conversation as we now understand conversation, and it
will probably concentrate on the humanity of Christ to
the exclusion of His deity. And, in fact, we find that
those Christians who attend solely to this first promise
always do fill it up with very earthly imagery indeed—
in fact with hymeneal or erotic imagery. I am not for a
moment condemning such imagery. I heartily wish I
could enter into it more deeply than I do, and pray that
I yet shall. But my point is that this also is only a symbol,
like the reality in some respects, but unlike it in others,
and therefore needs correction from the different symbols in the other promises. The variation of the promises
does not mean that anything other than God will be
our ultimate bliss; but because God is more than a
Person, and lest we should imagine the joy of His
presence too exclusively in terms of our present poor
experience of personal love, with all its narrowness and
strain and monotony, a dozen changing images cor-
recting and relieving each other, are supplied.

I turn next to the idea of glory. There is no getting
away from the fact that this idea is very prominent in the
New Testament and in early Christian writings. Salva-

tion is constantly associated with palms, crowns, white robes, thrones, and splendour like the sun and stars. All this makes no immediate appeal to me at all, and in that respect I fancy I am a typical modern. Glory suggests two ideas to me, of which one seems wicked and the other ridiculous. Either glory means to me fame, or it means luminosity. As for the first, since to be famous means to be better known than other people, the desire for fame appears to me as a competitive passion and therefore of hell rather than heaven. As for the second, who wishes to become a kind of living electric light bulb?

When I began to look into this matter I was shocked to find such different Christians as Milton, Johnson and Thomas Aquinas taking heavenly glory quite frankly in the sense of fame or good report. But not fame conferred by our fellow creatures—fame with God, approval or (I might say) " appreciation " by God. And then, when I had thought it over, I saw that this view was scriptural; nothing can eliminate from the parable the divine *accolade,* " Well done, thou good and faithful servant ". With that, a good deal of what I had been thinking all my life fell down like a house of cards. I suddenly remembered that no one can enter heaven except as a child; and nothing is so obvious in a child—not in a conceited child, but in a good child—as its great and undisguised pleasure in being praised. Not only in a child, either, but even in a dog or a horse. Apparently what I had mistaken for humility had, all these years, prevented me from understanding what is in fact the humblest, the most childlike, the most creaturely of pleasures—nay, the specific pleasure of the inferior : the pleasure of a beast before men, a child before its father, a pupil before his teacher, a creature before its Creator. I am not forgetting how horribly this most innocent desire is parodied in our human ambitions, or how very quickly, in my own experience, the lawful pleasure of praise from those whom it was my duty to please turns into the deadly poison of self-admiration. But I thought I could detect a moment—a very, very short moment—before this happened, during which the satisfaction of having pleased those whom I rightly loved and rightly feared was pure. And that is enough to raise our thoughts to what may happen when the redeemed soul, beyond all hope and nearly beyond belief, learns at last that she has pleased Him whom she was created to please. There will be no room for vanity then. She will be free from the miserable illusion that it is her doing. With no taint of what we should now call self-approval she will most innocently rejoice in the thing that God has made her to be, and the moment which heals her old inferiority complex for ever will also drown her pride deeper than Prospero's book. Perfect humility dispenses with modesty. If God is satisfied with the work, the work may be satisfied with itself; "it is not for her to bandy compliments with her Sovereign". I can imagine someone saying that he dislikes my idea of heaven as a place where we are patted on the back. But proud misunderstanding is behind that dislike. In the end that Face which is the delight or the terror of the universe must be turned upon each of us either with one expression or with the other, either conferring glory inexpressible or inflicting shame that can never be cured or disguised. I read in a periodical the other day that the fundamental thing is how we think of God. By God Himself, it is not! How God thinks of us is not only more important, but infinitely more important. Indeed, how we think of Him is of no importance except in so far as it is related to how He thinks of us. It is written that we shall "stand before" Him, shall appear, shall be inspected. The promise of glory is the promise, almost incredible and only possible by the work of Christ, that some of us, that any of us who really chooses, shall actually survive that examination, shall find approval, shall please God. To please God . . . to be a real ingredient in the divine happiness . . . to be loved by God, not merely pitied, but delighted in as an artist delights in his work or a father in a son—it seems impossible, a weight or burden of glory which our thoughts can hardly sustain. But so it is.

And now notice what is happening. If I had rejected the authoritative and scriptural image of glory and stuck obstinately to the vague desire which was, at the outset, my only pointer to heaven, I could have seen no connection at all between that desire and the Christian promise. But now, having followed up what seemed puzzling and repellent in the sacred books, I find, to my great surprise, looking back, that the connection is perfectly clear. Glory, as Christianity teaches me to hope for it, turns out to satisfy my original desire and indeed to reveal an element in that desire which I had not noticed. By ceasing for a moment to consider my own wants I have begun to learn better what I really wanted. When I attempted, a few minutes ago, to describe our spiritual longings, I was omitting one of their most curious characteristics. We usually notice it just as the moment of vision dies away, as the music ends or as the landscape loses the celestial light. What we feel then has been well described by Keats as "the journey homeward to habitual self". You know what I mean. For a few minutes we have had the illusion of belonging to that world.

Now we wake to find that it is no such thing. We have been mere spectators. Beauty has smiled, but not to welcome us; her face was turned in our direction, but not to see us. We have not been accepted, welcomed, or taken into the dance. We may go when we please, we may stay if we can: "Nobody marks us." A scientist may reply that since most of the things we call beautiful are inanimate, it is not very surprising that they take no notice of us. That, of course, is true. It is not the physical objects that I am speaking of, but that indescribable something of which they become for a moment the messengers. And part of the bitterness which mixes with the sweetness of that message is due to the fact that it so seldom seems to be a message intended for us, but rather something we have overheard. By bitterness I mean pain, not resentment. We should hardly dare to ask that any notice be taken of ourselves. But we pine. The sense that in this universe we are treated as strangers, the longing to be acknowledged, to meet with some response, to bridge some chasm that yawns between us and reality, is part of our inconsolable secret. And surely, from this point of view, the promise of glory, in the sense described, becomes highly relevant to our deep desire. For glory means good report with God, acceptance by God, response, acknowledgment, and welcome into the heart of things. The door on which we have been knocking all our lives will open at last.

Perhaps it seems rather crude to describe glory as the fact of being "noticed" by God. But this is almost the language of the New Testament. St. Paul promises to those who love God not, as we should expect, that they will know Him, but that they will be known by Him (I Cor. viii. 3). It is a strange promise. Does not God know all things at all times? But it is dreadfully re-echoed in another passage of the New Testament. There we are warned that it may happen to anyone of us to appear at last before the face of God and hear only the appalling words : " I never knew you. Depart from Me." In some sense, as dark to the intellect as it is unendurable to the feelings, we can be both banished from the presence of Him who is present everywhere and erased from the knowledge of Him who knows all. We can be left utterly and absolutely *outside*—repelled, exiled, estranged, finally and unspeakably ignored. On the other hand, we can be called in, welcomed, received, acknowledged. We walk every day on the razor edge between these two incredible possibilities. Apparently, then, our lifelong nostalgia, our longing to be reunited with something in the universe from which we now feel cut off, to be on the inside of some door which we have always seen from the outside, is no mere neurotic fancy, but the truest index of our real situation. And to be at last summoned inside would be both glory and honour beyond all our merits and also the healing of that old ache.

And this brings me to the other sense of glory—glory as brightness, splendour, luminosity. We are to shine as the sun, we are to be given the Morning Star. I think I begin to see what it means. In one way, of course, God has given us the Morning Star already : you can go and enjoy the gift on many fine mornings if you get up early enough. What more, you may ask, do we want? Ah, but we want so much more—something the books on æsthetics take little notice of. But the poets and the mythologies know all about it. We do not want merely to *see* beauty, though, God knows, even that is bounty enough.

We want something else which can hardly be put into words—to be united with the beauty we see, to pass into it, to receive it into ourselves, to bathe in it, to become part of it. That is why we have peopled air and earth and water with gods and goddesses and nymphs and elves—that, though we cannot, yet these projections can, enjoy in themselves that beauty, grace, and power of which Nature is the image. That is why the poets tell us such lovely falsehoods. They talk as if the west wind could really sweep into a human soul; but it can't. They tell us that "beauty born of murmuring sound" will pass into a human face; but it won't. Or not yet. For if we take the imagery of Scripture seriously, if we believe that God will one day *give* us the Morning Star and cause us to *put on* the splendour of the sun, then we may surmise that both the ancient myths and the modern poetry, so false as history, may be very near the truth as prophecy. At present we are on the outside of the world, the wrong side of the door. We discern the freshness and purity of morning, but they do not make us fresh and pure. We cannot mingle with the splendours we see. But all the leaves of the New Testament are rustling with the rumour that it will not always be so. Some day, God willing, we shall get *in*. When human souls have become as perfect in voluntary obedience as the inanimate creation is in its lifeless obedience, then they will put on its glory, or rather that greater glory of which Nature is only the first sketch. For you must not think that I am putting forward any heathen fancy of being absorbed into Nature. Nature is mortal; we shall outlive her. When all the suns and nebulæ have passed away, each one of you will still be alive. Nature is only the image, the symbol; but it is the symbol Scripture invites me to use. We are summoned to pass in through Nature, beyond her, into that splendour which she fitfully reflects.

And in there, in beyond Nature, we shall eat of the tree of life. At present, if we are reborn in Christ, the spirit in us lives directly on God; but the mind, and still more the body, receives life from Him at a thousand removes —through our ancestors, through our food, through the elements. The faint, far-off results of those energies which God's creative rapture implanted in matter when He made the worlds are what we now call physical pleasures; and even thus filtered, they are too much for our present management. What would it be to taste at the fountain-head that stream of which even these lower reaches prove so intoxicating? Yet that, I believe, is what lies before us. The whole man is to drink joy from the fountain of joy. As St. Augustine said, the rapture of the saved soul will "flow over" into the glorified body. In the light of our present specialised and depraved appetites we cannot imagine this *torrens voluptatis,* and I warn everyone most seriously not to try. But it must be mentioned, to drive out thoughts even more misleading—thoughts that what is saved is a mere ghost, or that the risen body lives in numb insensibility. The body was made for the Lord, and these dismal fancies are wide of the mark.

Meanwhile the cross comes before the crown and to-morrow is a Monday morning. A cleft has opened in the pitiless walls of the world, and we are invited to follow our great Captain inside. The following Him is, of course, the essential point. That being so, it may be asked what practical use there is in the speculations which I have been indulging. I can think of at least one such use. It may be possible for each to think too much of his own potential glory hereafter; it is hardly possible for him to think too often or too deeply about that of his neighbour. The load, or weight, or burden of my neighbour's glory should be laid daily on my back, a load so heavy that only humility can carry it, and the backs of the proud will be broken. It is a serious thing to live in a society of possible gods and goddesses, to remember that the dullest and most uninteresting person you can talk to may one day be a creature which, if you saw it now, you would be strongly tempted to worship, or else a horror and a corruption such as you now meet, if at all, only in a nightmare. All day long we are, in some degree, helping each other to one or other of these destinations. It is in the light of these overwhelming possibilities, it is with the awe and the circumspection proper to them, that we should conduct all our dealings with one another, all friendships, all loves, all play, all politics. There are no *ordinary* people. You have never talked to a mere mortal. Nations, cultures, arts, civilisations—these are mortal, and their life is to ours as the life of a gnat. But it is immortals whom we joke with, work with, marry, snub, and exploit—immortal horrors or everlasting splendours. This does not mean that we are to be perpetually solemn. We must play. But our merriment must be of that kind (and it is, in fact, the merriest kind) which exists between people who have, from the outset, taken each other seriously—no flippancy, no superiority, no presumption. And our charity must be a real and costly love, with deep feeling for the sins in spite of which we love the sinner—no mere tolerance, or indulgence which parodies love as flippancy parodies merriment. Next to the Blessed Sacrament itself, your neighbour is the holiest object presented to your senses. If he is your Christian neighbour he is holy in almost the same way, for in him the Christ *vere latitat*—the glorifier and the glorified, Glory Himself—is truly hidden.

A Sermon at the Church of St. Mary the Virgin, Oxford

GOOD WORK AND GOOD WORKS

" Good works " in the plural is an expression much more familiar to modern Christendom than "good work". Good works are chiefly alms-giving or "helping" in the parish. They are quite separate from one's "work". And good works need not be good work, as anyone can see by inspecting some of the objects made to be sold at bazaars for charitable purposes. This is not according to our example. When our Lord provided a poor wedding party with an extra glass of wine all round, he was doing good works. But also good work; it was a wine really worth drinking. Nor is the neglect of goodness in our " work ", our job, according to precept. The apostle says everyone must not only work but work to produce what is " good ".

The idea of Good Work is not quite extinct among us, though it is not, I fear, especially characteristic of religious people. I have found it among cabinet-makers, cobblers, and sailors. It is no use at all trying to impress sailors with a new liner because she is the biggest or costliest ship afloat. They look for what they call her "lines": they predict how she will behave in a heavy sea. Artists also talk of Good Work; but decreasingly. They begin to prefer words like "significant", "important", "contemporary", or "daring". These are not, to my mind, good symptoms.

But the great mass of men in all fully industrialised societies are the victims of a situation which almost excludes the idea of Good Work from the outset. "Built-in obsolescence " becomes an economic necessity. Unless an article is so made that it will go to pieces in a year or two and thus have to be replaced, you will not get a sufficient turnover. A hundred years ago, when a man got married, he had built for him (if he were rich enough) a carriage in which he expected to drive for the rest of his life. He now buys a car which he expects to sell again in two years. Work nowadays must *not* be good.

For the wearer, zip fasteners have this advantage over buttons : that, while they last, they will save him an infinitesimal amount of time and trouble. For the producer, they have a much more solid merit; they don't remain in working order long. Bad work is the *desideratum*.

We must avoid taking a glibly moral view of this situation. It is not solely the result of original or actual sin. It has stolen upon us, unforeseen and unintended. The degraded commercialism of our minds is quite as much its result as its cause. Nor can it, in my opinion, be cured by purely moral efforts.

Originally things are made for use, or delight, or (more often) for both. The savage hunter makes himself a weapon of flint or bone; makes it as well as he can, for if it is blunt or brittle he will kill no meat. His woman makes a clay pot to fetch water in; again as well as she can, for she will have to use it. But they do not for long (if at all) abstain from decorating these things; they want to have (like Dogberry) " everything handsome about them ". And while they work, we may be sure they sing or whistle or at least hum. They may tell stories too.

Into this situation, unobtrusive as Eden's snake and at first as innocent as that snake once was, there must sooner

or later come a change. Each family no longer makes all
it needs. There is a specialist, a potter making pots for
the whole village, a smith making weapons for all; a
bard (poet and musician in one) singing and story-telling
for all. It is significant that in Homer the smith of the
gods is lame, and the poet among men is blind. That
may be how the thing began. The defectives, who are no
use as hunters or warriors, may be set aside to provide
both necessaries and recreation for those who are.

The importance of this change is that we now have
people making things (pots, swords, lays) not for their
own use and delight but for the use and delight of others.
And of course they must, in some way or other, be rewarded for doing it. The change is necessary unless
society and arts are to remain in a state not of paradisal,
but of feeble, blundering, and impoverishing simplicity.
It is kept healthy by two facts. First, these specialists
will do their work as well as they can. They are right up
against the people who are going to use it. You'll have all
the women in the village after you if you make bad pots.
You'll be shouted down if you sing a dull lay. If you
make bad swords, then at best the warriors will come
back and thrash you; at worst, they won't come back at
all, for the enemy will have killed them, and your village
will be burned and you yourself enslaved or knocked on
the head. And secondly, because the specialists are doing
as well as they can something that is indisputably worth
doing, they will delight in their work. We must not
idealise. It will not all be delight. The smith may be
overworked. The bard may be frustrated when the
village insists on hearing his last lay over again (or a new
one exactly like it) while he is longing to get a hearing
for some wonderful innovation. But, by and large, the

specialists have a life fit for a man; usefulness, a reasonable amount of honour, and the joy of exercising skill.

I lack space and, of course, knowledge, to trace the whole process from this state of affairs to that in which we are living to-day. But I think we can now disengage the essence of the change. Granted the departure from the primitive condition in which everyone makes things for himself, and granted, therefore, a condition in which many work for others (who will pay them), there are still two sorts of job. Of one sort, a man can truly say, " I am doing work which is worth doing. It would still be worth doing if nobody paid for it. But as I have no private means, and need to be fed and housed and clothed, I must be paid while I do it." The other kind of job is that in which people do work whose sole purpose is the earning of money : work which need not be, ought not to be, or would not be, done by anyone in the whole world unless it were paid.

We may thank God there are still plenty of jobs in the first category. The agricultural labourer, the policeman, the doctor, the artist, the teacher, the priest, and many others, are doing what is worth doing in itself; what quite a number of people would do, and do, without pay; what every family would attempt to do for itself, in some amateurish fashion, if it lived in primitive isolation. Of course jobs of this kind need not be agreeable. Ministering to a leper settlement is one of them.

The opposite extreme may be represented by two examples. I do not necessarily equate them morally, but they are alike by our present classification. One is the work of the professional prostitute. The peculiar horror of her work—if you say we should not call it work, think again—the thing that makes it so much more horrible than ordinary fornication, is that it is an extreme example of an activity which has no possible end in view except money. You cannot go further in that direction than sexual intercourse, not only without marriage, not only without love, but even without lust. My other example is this. I often see a hoarding which bears a notice to the effect that thousands look at this space and your firm ought to hire it for an advertisement of its wares. Consider by how many stages this is separated from " making that which is good ". A carpenter has made this hoarding; that, in itself, has no use. Printers and paper-makers have worked to produce the notice —worthless until someone hires the space—worthless to him until he pastes on it another notice, still worthless to him unless it persuades someone else to buy his goods; which themselves may be ugly, useless, and pernicious luxuries that no mortal would have bought unless the advertisement, by its sexy or snobbish incantations, had conjured up in him a factitious desire for them. At every stage of the process, work is being done whose sole value lies in the money it brings.

Such would seem to be the inevitable result of a society which depends predominantly on buying and selling. In a rational world, things would be made because they were wanted; in the actual world, wants have to be created in order that people may receive money for making the things. That is why the distrust or contempt of trade which we find in earlier societies should not be too hastily set down as mere snobbery. The more important trade is, the more people are condemned to—and, worse still, learn to prefer—what we have called the second kind of job. Work worth doing apart from its pay, enjoyable work, and good work become the privilege of a fortunate minority. The competitive search for customers dominates international situations.

Within my lifetime in England money was (very properly) collected to buy shirts for some men who were out of work. The work they were out of was the manufacture of shirts.

That such a state of affairs cannot be permanent is easily foreseen. But unfortunately it is most likely to perish by its own internal contradictions in a manner which will cause immense suffering. It can be ended painlessly only if we find some way of ending it voluntarily; and needless to say I have no plan for doing that, and none of our masters—the Big Men behind government and industry—would take any notice if I had. The only hopeful sign at the moment is the "space-race" between America and Russia. Since we have got ourselves into a state where the main problem is not to provide people with what they need or like, but to keep people making things (it hardly matters what), great powers could not easily be better employed than in fabricating costly objects which they then fling overboard. It keeps money circulating and factories working, and it won't do space much harm—or not for a long time. But the relief is partial and temporary. The main practical task for most of us is not to give the Big Men advice about how to end our fatal economy—we have none to give and they wouldn't listen—but to consider how we can live within it as little hurt and degraded as possible.

It is something even to recognise that it is fatal and insane. Just as the Christian has a great advantage over other men, not by being less fallen than they nor less doomed to live in a fallen world, but by knowing that he *is* a fallen man in a fallen world; so we shall do better if we remember at every moment what Good Work was and how impossible it has now become for the majority. We may have to earn our living by taking part in the production of objects which are rotten in quality and which, even if they were good in quality, would not be worth producing—the demand or "market" for them having been simply engineered by advertisement. Beside the waters of Babylon—or the assembly belt—we shall still say inwardly, "If I forget thee, O Jerusalem, may my right hand forget its cunning." (It will.)

And of course we shall keep our eyes skinned for any chance of escape. If we have any "choice of a career" (but has one man in a thousand any such thing?) we shall be after the sane jobs like greyhounds and stick there like limpets. We shall try, if we get the chance, to earn our living by doing well what would be worth doing even if we had not our living to earn. A considerable mortification of our avarice may be necessary. It is usually the insane jobs that lead to big money; they are often also the least laborious.

But beyond all this there is something subtler. We must take great care to preserve our habits of mind from infection by those which the situation has bred. Such an infection has, in my opinion, deeply corrupted our artists.

Until quite recently—until the latter part of the last century—it was taken for granted that the business of the artist was to delight and instruct his public. There were, of course, different publics; the street-songs and the oratorios were not addressed to the same audience (though I think a good many people liked both). And an artist might lead his public on to appreciate finer things than they had wanted at first; but he could do this only by being, from the first, if not merely entertaining, yet entertaining, and if not completely intelligible, yet very largely intelligible. All this has changed. In the highest æsthetic circles one now hears nothing about the artist's duty to us. It is all about our duty to him. He owes us nothing; we owe him " recognition ", even though he has never paid the slightest attention to our tastes, interests, or habits. If we don't give it to him, our name is mud. In this shop, the customer is always wrong.

But this change is surely part of our changed attitude to all work. As " giving employment " becomes more important than making things men need or like, there is a tendency to regard every trade as something that exists chiefly for the sake of those who practise it. The smith does not work in order that the warriors may fight; the warriors exist and fight in order that the smith may be kept busy. The bard does not exist in order to delight the tribe : the tribe exists in order to appreciate the bard.

In industry highly creditable motives, as well as insanity, lie behind this change of attitude. A real advance in charity stopped us talking about " surplus population " and started us talking instead about " unemployment ". The danger is that this should lead us to forget that employment is not an end in itself. We want people to be employed only as a means to their being fed—believing (whether rightly, who knows?) that it is better to feed them for making things badly than for doing nothing.

But though we have a duty to feed the hungry, I doubt whether we have a duty to " appreciate " the ambitious. This attitude to art is fatal to good work. Many modern novels, poems, and pictures, which we are browbeaten into " appreciating ", are not good work because they are not *work* at all. They are mere puddles of spilled sensibility or reflection. When an artist is in the

strict sense working, he of course takes into account the
existing taste, interests, and capacity of his audience.
These, no less than the language, the marble, or the
paint, are part of his raw material; to be used, tamed,
sublimated, not ignored nor defied. Haughty indiffer-
ence to them is not genius nor integrity; it is laziness and
incompetence. You have not learned your job. Hence,
real honest-to-God work, so far as the arts are concerned,
now appears chiefly in low-brow art; in the film, the
detective story, the children's story. These are often
sound structures; seasoned wood, accurately dovetailed,
the stresses all calculated; skill and labour successfully
used to do what is intended. Do not misunderstand. The
high-brow productions may, of course, reveal a finer
sensibility and profounder thought. But a puddle is not a
work, whatever rich wines or oils or medicines have gone
into it.

" Great works " (of art) and " good works " (of charity)
had better also be Good Work. Let choirs sing well or
not at all. Otherwise we merely confirm the majority in
their conviction that the world of Business, which does
with such efficiency so much that never really needed
doing is the real, the adult, and the practical world; and
that all this " culture " and all this " religion " (horrid
words both) are essentially marginal, amateurish, and
rather effeminate activities.

When a layman has to preach a sermon I think he is most likely to be useful, or even interesting, if he starts exactly from where he is himself; not so much presuming to instruct as comparing notes.

Not long ago when I was using the collect for the fourth Sunday after Trinity in my private prayers I found that I had made a slip of the tongue. I had meant to pray that I might so pass through things temporal that I finally lost not the things eternal; I found I had prayed so to pass through things eternal that I finally lost not the things temporal. Of course I don't think that a slip of the tongue is a sin. I am not sure that I am even a strict enough Freudian to believe that all such slips, without exception, are deeply significant. But I think some of them are significant, and I thought this was one of that sort. I thought that what I had inadvertently said very nearly expressed something I had really wished.

Very nearly; not, of course, precisely. I had never been quite stupid enough to think that the eternal could, strictly, be " passed through ". What I had wanted to pass through without prejudice to my things temporal was those hours or moments in which I attended to the eternal, in which I exposed myself to it.

I mean this sort of thing. I say my prayers, I read a book of devotion, I prepare for, or receive, the Sacrament. But while I do these things there is, so to speak, a voice inside me that urges caution. It tells me to be careful; to keep my head; not to go too far; not to burn my boats. I come into the presence of God with a great fear lest anything should happen to me within that presence which will prove too intolerably inconvenient when I have come out again into my " ordinary " life. I don't want to be carried away into any resolution which I shall afterwards regret. For I know I shall be feeling quite different after breakfast; I don't want anything to happen to me at the altar which will run up too big a bill to pay then. It would be very disagreeable, for instance, to take the duty of charity (while I am at the altar) so seriously that, after breakfast, I had to tear up the really stunning reply I had written to an impudent correspondent yesterday and meant to post to-day. It would be very tiresome to commit myself to a programme of temperance which would cut off my after-breakfast cigarette (or, at best, make it cruelly alternative to a cigarette later in the morning). Even repentance of past acts will have to be paid for. By repenting one acknowledges them as sins—therefore not to be repeated. Better leave that issue undecided.

The root principle of all these precautions is the same: to guard the things temporal. And I find some evidence that this temptation is not peculiar to me. A good author (whose name I have forgotten) asks somewhere, " Have we never risen from our knees in haste for fear God's will should become too unmistakable if we prayed longer?" The following story was told as true. An Irishwoman who had just been at confession met on the steps of the chapel the other woman who was her greatest enemy in the village. The other woman let fly a torrent of abuse. " Isn't it a shame for ye," replied Biddy, " to be talking to me like that, ye coward, and me in a state of Grace the way I can't answer ye? But you wait. I won't be in a state of Grace long." There is an excellent tragi-comic example in Trollope's *Last Chronicle*. The Archdeacon was angry with his eldest son. He at once made a number of legal arrangements to the son's disadvantage. They could all easily have been made a few days later, but Trollope explains why the Archdeacon would not wait. To reach the next day, he had to pass through his evening prayers, and he knew that he might not be able to carry his hostile plans safely through the clause, "Forgive us our tresspasses as we forgive." So he got in first, he decided to present God with a *fait accompli*. This is an extreme case of the precautions I am talking about; the man will not venture within reach of the eternal until he has made the things temporal safe in advance.

This is my endlessly recurrent temptation: to go down to that Sea (I think St. John of the Cross called God a sea) and there neither dive nor swim nor float, but only dabble and splash, careful not to get out of my depth and holding on to the lifeline which connects me with my things temporal.

It is different from the temptations that met us at the beginning of the Christian life. Then we fought (at least I fought) against admitting the claims of the eternal at all. And when we had fought, and been beaten, and surrendered, we supposed that all would be fairly plain sailing. This temptation comes later. It is addressed to those who have already admitted the claim in principle and are even making some sort of effort to meet it. Our temptation is to look eagerly for the minimum that will be accepted. We are in fact very like honest but reluctant taxpayers. We approve of an income tax in principle. We make our returns truthfully. But we dread a rise in the tax. We are very careful to pay no more than is necessary. And we hope—we very ardently hope— that after we have paid it there will still be enough left to live on.

And notice that those cautions which the tempter whispers in our ears are all plausible. Indeed, I don't think he often tries to deceive us (after early youth) with a direct lie. The plausibility is this. It is really possible to be carried away by religious emotion – *enthusiasm* as our ancestors called it—into resolutions and attitudes which we shall, not sinfully but rationally, not when we are more worldly but when we are wiser, have cause to regret. We can become scrupulous or fanatical; we can, in what seems zeal but is really presumption, embrace tasks never intended for us. That is the truth in the temptation. The lie consists in the suggestion that our best protection is a prudent regard for the safety of our pocket, our habitual indulgences, and our ambitions. But that is quite false. Our real protection is to be sought elsewhere; in common Christian usage, in moral theology, in steady rational thinking, in the advice of good friends and good books, and (if need be) in a skilled spiritual director. Swimming lessons are better than a life-line to the shore.

For of course that life-line is really a death-line. There is no parallel to paying taxes and living on the remainder. For it is not so much of our time and so much of our attention that God demands; it is not even all our time and all our attention : it is our selves. For each of us the Baptist's words are true : " He must increase and I decrease." He will be infinitely merciful to our repeated failures; I know no promise that he will accept a deliber- ate compromise. For He has, in the last resort, nothing to give us but Himself; and He can give that only in so far as our self-affirming will retires and makes room for Him in our souls. Let us make up our minds to it; there will be nothing " of our own " left over to live on; no " ordinary " life. I do not mean that each of us will necessarily be called to be a martyr or even an ascetic. That's as may be. For some (nobody knows which) the Christian life will include much leisure, many occupations we naturally like. But these will be received from God's hands. In a perfect Christian they would be as much part of his " religion ", his " service ", as his hardest duties, and his feasts would be as Christian as his fasts. What cannot be admitted—what must exist only as an undefeated but daily resisted enemy—is the idea of something that is " our own ", some area in which we are to be " out of school ", on which God has no claim.

For he claims all, because He is love and must bless. He cannot bless us unless he has us. When we try to keep within us an area that is our own, we try to keep an area of death. Therefore, in love, He claims all. There's no bargaining with Him.

This is, I take it, the meaning of all those sayings that alarm me most. Thomas More said, " If ye make indentures with God how much ye will serve Him, ye shall find ye have signed both of them yourself." Law, in his terrible, cool voice, said, " Many will be rejected at the last day, not because they have taken no time or pains about their salvation, but because they have not taken time and pains enough;" and later, in his richer, Behmenite period, " If you have not chosen the Kingdom of God, it will make in the end no difference what you have chosen instead." Those are hard words to take. Will it really make no difference whether it was women or patriotism, cocaine or art, whisky or a seat in the Cabinet, money or science? Well, surely no difference that matters. We shall have missed the end for which we are formed and rejected the only thing that satisfies. Does it matter to a man dying in a desert, by which choice of route he missed the only well?

It is a remarkable fact that on this subject Heaven and Hell speak with one voice. The tempter tells me, " Take care. Think how much this good resolve, the acceptance of this Grace, is going to cost." But Our Lord equally tells us to count the cost. Even in human affairs great importance is attached to the agreement of those whose testimony hardly ever agrees. Here, more. Between them it would seem to be pretty clear that paddling is of little consequence. What matters, what Heaven desires and Hell fears, is precisely that further step; out of our depth, out of our own control.

And yet, I am not in despair. At this point I become what some would call very Evangelical; at any rate very un-Pelagian. I do not think any efforts of my own will can end once and for all this craving for limited liabilities, this fatal reservation, only God can. I have good faith and hope He will. Of course I don't mean that I can therefore, as they say, " sit back ". What God does for us, He does in us. The process of doing it will appear to me (and not falsely) to be the daily or hourly repeated exercises of my own will in renouncing this attitude; especially each morning, for it grows all over me like a new shell each night. Failures will be forgiven; it is acquiescence that is fatal, the permitted, regularised presense of an area in ourselves which we still claim for our own. We may never, this side of death, drive the invader out of our territory; but we must be in the Resistance, not in the Vichy government. And this, so far as I can yet see, must be begun again every day. Our morning prayer should be that in the *Imitation: Da hodie perfecte incipere*—grant me to make an unflawed beginning to-day, for I have done nothing yet.

A Sermon at Magdalene College, Cambridge

Also available in Fount Paperbacks

BOOKS BY DAVID KOSSOFF

Bible Stories

'To my mind there is no doubt that these stories make the Bible come alive. Mr Kossoff is a born storyteller. He has the gift of making the old stories new.'

William Barclay

The Book of Witnesses

'The little stories are fascinating in the warm humanity they reveal. Right from the first one the reader is enthralled . . . bringing the drama of the New Testament into our daily lives with truly shattering impact.'

Religious Book News

The Voices of Masada

'This is imaginative historical writing of the highest standard.'

Church Times

The Little Book of Sylvanus

Sylvanus, the quiet, observant man, tells his version of the events surrounding the 'carpenter preacher' of Nazareth, from the Crucifixion to Pentecost. A moving and unforgettable view of the gospel story, and a sequel to *The Book of Witnesses*.

Fount Paperbacks

Fount is one of the leading paperback publishers of religious books and below are some of its recent titles.

☐ GETHSEMANE Martin Israel £2.50
☐ HIS HEALING TOUCH Michael Buckley £2.50
☐ YES TO LIFE David Clarke £2.95
☐ THE DIVORCED CATHOLIC Edmund Flood £1.95
☐ THE WORLD WALKS BY Sue Masham £2.95
☐ C. S. LEWIS: THE MAN AND HIS GOD
  Richard Harries £1.75
☐ BEING FRIENDS Peter Levin £2.95
☐ DON'T BE AFRAID TO SAY YOU'RE LONELY
  Christopher Martin £2.50
☐ BASIL HUME: A PORTRAIT Tony Castle (ed.) £3.50
☐ TERRY WAITE: MAN WITH A MISSION
  Trevor Barnes £2.95
☐ PRAYING THROUGH PARADOX Charles Elliott £2.50
☐ TIMELESS AT HEART C. S. Lewis £2.50
☐ THE POLITICS OF PARADISE Frank Field £3.50
☐ THE WOUNDED CITY Trevor Barnes £2.50
☐ THE SACRAMENT OF THE WORD Donald Coggan £2.95
☐ IS THERE ANYONE THERE? Richard MacKenna £1.95

All Fount paperbacks are available through your bookshop or newsagent, or they can be ordered by post from Fount Paperbacks, Cash Sales Department, G.P.O. Box 29, Douglas, Isle of Man. Please send purchase price plus 22p per book, maximum postage £3. Customers outside the UK send purchase price, plus 22p per book. Cheque, postal order or money order. No currency.

NAME (Block letters)_____

ADDRESS _____

_____

_____